THE ROGUISH BARON

SOPHIE BARNES

THE ROGUISH BARON

Diamonds in the Rough

Cover Design by The Killion Group, Inc.

Novels

The Brazen Beauties
Mr. Dale and The Divorcée

Diamonds in the Rough
The Dishonored Viscount
Her Scottish Scoundrel
The Formidable Earl
The Forgotten Duke
The Infamous Duchess
The Illegitimate Duke
The Duke of Her Desire
A Most Unlikely Duke

The Crawfords
Her Seafaring Scoundrel
More Than a Rogue
No Ordinary Duke

Secrets at Thorncliff Manor
Christmas at Thorncliff Manor

His Scandalous Kiss

The Earl's Complete Surrender

Lady Sarah's Sinful Desires

At The Kingsborough Ball

The Danger in Tempting an Earl

The Scandal in Kissing an Heir

The Trouble with Being a Duke

The Summersbys

The Secret Life of Lady Lucinda

There's Something About Lady Mary

Lady Alexandra's Excellent Adventure

Standalone Titles

Sealed With A Yuletide Kiss (An Historical Romance Advent Calendar)

The Girl Who Stepped Into The Past

How Miss Rutherford Got Her Groove Back

Novellas

The Enterprising Scoundrels

Mr. Donahue's Total Surrender

Diamonds in the Rough

The Roguish Baron

The Townsbridges

An Unexpected Temptation

A Duke for Miss Townsbridge

Falling for Mr. Townsbridge

Lady Abigail's Perfect Match

When Love Leads To Scandal

Once Upon a Townsbridge Story

The Honorable Scoundrels

The Duke Who Came To Town

The Earl Who Loved Her

The Governess Who Captured His Heart

Standalone Titles

The Secrets of Colchester Hall

Miss Compton's Christmas Romance

Mistletoe Magic (from Five Golden Rings: A Christmas Collection)

CHAPTER ONE

Ramcroft, 1823

"Jack's coming home."

Sophia's pulse leapt in response to the words being spoken. She did not want to relish the news her friends were sharing, nor did she wish to look forward to the coming weeks with eager expectation. Jack Lancaster, Baron Hawthorne, did not deserve to be pined for. She ought to forget him. And yet...

"When is your brother due to arrive?" Her stomach fluttered in anticipation of what Jack's sisters might say. At the age of twenty, the twins were only two years younger than Sophia, and although they were the daughters of an earl while she was nothing more than the local vicar's foster child, they'd played together often while growing up and had remained close into adulthood.

Felicity, the more vocal twin, leaned forward. Unlike her sister, Kaitlin, whose hair was as black as Jack's, Felicity had their mother's auburn curls. "Tomorrow, so he can get settled before the rest of the guests arrive for the house party."

The house party had been their father's idea. Apparently, after declaring his daughters' debuts and subsequent Season a failure, he'd invited five gentlemen to visit his home for the next few weeks. The intention behind it was obvious and had caused both Felicity and Kaitlin to look uncomfortable when they'd mentioned it to Sophia during their last get-together.

"So soon?" Sophia clutched her cup and tried to ignore the frantic beat of her heart.

"We're hoping you'll join us for dinner on Saturday," Kaitlin said with a gentle smile. "So we'll not have to face all the men Mama and Papa have invited alone."

Sophia took a hasty sip of her tea. See Jack? Dine with him at Eastgate Abbey? Relive the pain of his indifference?

She'd rather toss herself into a frozen lake.

"Thank you," she told her friends, her voice not nearly as firm as she wished, "but I fear I must decline."

Felicity and Kaitlin shared a look. They flattened their mouths and straightened their backs. Whatever levity they'd shown before vanished beneath a layer of determination.

Sophia steeled herself.

"We thought you might," Felicity said.

"So we made a plan," Kaitlin added.

Unease slid down Sophia's spine. "How do you mean?"

"Well, we think it would be splendid if you and Jack were to marry," Felicity said.

Sophia stared at her friend. Her grip on her teacup tightened. "No."

"But you've been in love with him since forever," Kaitlin said.

"Feelings change," Sophia said.

"Have yours?" Felicity asked.

She wanted to say yes and deny the yearnings of her heart, but she couldn't. Felicity and Kaitlin were her dearest friends, and she'd never lied to them about anything. "No."

"Good. Because we would like nothing better than for you to become our sister." Felicity smiled while Kaitlin snatched up a biscuit and bit it in half.

Sophia sighed. "He doesn't see me as a potential match and never will. For a good reason, if I may remind you."

"I disagree," Felicity said. "Mama and Papa have both welcomed you into our home."

"As your friend," Sophia pointed out. "Not as a candidate for the future Lady Hawthorne. No upstanding family would ever approve of their child marrying down."

"You're the best person there is," Kaitlin argued.

"I am an orphan with no connections." Sophia shook her head. She'd always known she was a fool for dreaming of Jack.

"That's not true," Felicity said. "Mr. and Mrs. Fenmore are both highly respected."

"As they should be, but neither of them is my relation." Sophia closed her eyes briefly against the reality of her situation. The vicar and his wife had raised her after finding her inside their church. According to what they'd told her, she'd managed to topple the basket she'd been in, and was tangled in her blanket on the cold stone floor. Her desperate cries had gone straight to the Fenmore's hearts. And although they'd already had a son of their own, they'd never made a distinction between her and Edward, had raised them as though they were siblings by birth. She had nothing but love for them, but that didn't mean she was blind to her situation.

"Semantics," Felicity said as if she could brush aside every rule upon which Society rested. "We know you and Jack would be perfect together. Hence the plan."

Against her better judgment, Sophia decided to humor her. "What does this plan of yours involve?"

"Getting Jack to pull his head out of his—"

"Kaitlin," Felicity chastised. She gave her younger sister a hard look, then turned her attention back to Sophia. "It is our belief that Jack could be persuaded to make you an offer of marriage."

"How romantic," Sophia muttered. "Perhaps we should tie him up too and force him to speak his vows?"

"Based on observation," Felicity went on, ignoring Sophia's remark, "he cares for you a great deal."

"I disagree." The manner in which they'd last parted had proven the opposite. But Sophia had never shared Jack's last words to her with anyone. Instead, she'd carried that pain alone.

"He never kept us company growing up, unless you happened to be there," Kaitlin said. "And after he went away to school, he'd always ask after you when he visited, until we invited you over."

"Once you arrived, he'd light up," Felicity said. "Have you forgotten how close the two of you were with your inside jokes and the way you'd always finish each other's sentences?"

A knot formed in Sophia's breast. Her fondest memories were of Jack, of him teaching her how to whistle, of the two of them fishing together while Kaitlin and Felicity chose to pick berries with Edward. Jack had even shown her how to whittle, allowing her to make a few cuts on the wooden rabbit he'd later gifted her for her birthday. The small figurine was her most prized possession.

Later, when Jack came home on holiday from Eton, they discussed his studies at length. The five years between them had never seemed to matter. And since she'd always read up on politics and philosophy during his absence, she'd been prepared to discuss his subjects of choice. She'd even kept abreast of all the news, just for the pleasure of seeing the look of surprise in his eyes when she referenced a bill passed in Parliament or some new scientific discovery.

"That was a long time ago," Sophia said in response to Felicity's question. "It's been four years since Jack's last visit to these parts."

Kaitlin knit her brow. "Has it really?"

"During which we've not been in touch at all." Sophia set her cup aside and folded her hands in her lap. "A lot can happen in four years. I do read the gossip column, in case you weren't aware. So I know of Jack's reputation."

"Journalists write a great deal of things," Felicity said. "It isn't always true."

"And even if it were," Kaitlin put in, "I don't see the issue. After all, Jack's hardly the first man to have a few dalliances on his way toward matrimonial bliss."

Sophia raised her eyebrows. "He's been labeled a rake."

"A misunderstanding, I'm sure," Felicity said with absolute loyalty.

It was what Sophia hoped for too since she didn't want to think less of the man she'd always held in such high regard. Still, the numerous accounts of him flirting with one debutante after another, of dancing daringly close with some and casting wicked glances at others, of changing mistresses so frequently she'd lost track, and of having affairs with other men's wives, was cause for great concern.

"You'll see," Kaitlin said.

"Please change your mind about dinner," Felicity pressed. "I know Jack would be thrilled to reconnect with you. And if you agree to our plan, then—"

"You've still not told me what this plan of yours entails," Sophia said. As much as she loathed the idea of trying to sway Jack's intentions toward her, she couldn't stop her curiosity.

"We believe Jack has been taking you for granted," Kaitlin said. "You've always been here, unattached, waiting for his return."

"But what if that were to change?" Felicity asked. "What if when Jack arrives on Friday, you've already been spoken for?"

Sophia's heart jolted. "What are you talking about?"

"Since our debuts last year, we've realized something." Kaitlin glanced at Felicity before she said, "Men tend to have greater interest in a woman if other men are vying for her hand. It's almost as if they suddenly notice her."

"Which is why we've spoken with Edward," Felicity said.

Sophia's jaw dropped. "You've what?"

"It made sense to find out if he was willing to help before we mentioned the idea to you, and he has agreed."

A new sort of panic swept through Sophia, brought on by the prospect of actually going through with this harebrained scheme. Edward was like a brother. She'd grown up alongside him. The idea of even feigning a courtship with him felt wrong. So it shocked her to learn he would do so since she was certain he must feel the same.

"I'm not the least bit comfortable with this," she said. "It's deceptive. What if someone gets hurt? Never mind the fact that I don't believe your parents would give their blessing even if Jack were to propose. Which I doubt he will since he doesn't love me in return."

"That's where we disagree," Felicity said. "Kaitlin and I are of the opinion that Jack does love you but that he just hasn't realized it yet. All we want to do is give him a nudge - a chance for him to come to terms with the contents of his heart before it's too late."

"Too late?" Sophia spoke the words with difficulty.

Felicity tilted her head. "You are two and twenty years of age, Sophia. How much longer do you think it will be before the Fenmores insist you marry?"

"I haven't really thought about that," Sophia told her. "It isn't something we've discussed and with the murkiness surrounding my birth taken into account, I never really considered…"

"Perhaps you should," Kaitlin told her gently.

Sophia supposed her friend was correct. She'd just gotten used to the way things were. A thought struck and she bit her lip as she pondered the recent church services she had attended with the Fenmores. They'd both been eager to introduce her to some of the local young men - a couple of farmers and the newly arrived school teacher. Furthermore, they were singing Edward's praises to her every day now. Only she'd not put much weight in any of it until this very moment.

Had they been actively trying to bring about a courtship?

If so, then that had to mean they expected her to start thinking of marriage. Even if they'd not yet told her so directly.

She sank against her seat with a long exhale. Had she been two years younger, like Felicity and Kaitlin, and in their social position, she would have been presented at court. Parties would have been hosted in her name in an effort to find her a husband.

Sophia's insides tightened as she considered the

pressure Felicity and Kaitlin must be under. And as their friend, ought she not be there to offer support, regardless of whether or not she was forced to face Jack?

A deep inhale and the subsequent exhale brought her duty toward them into focus.

"Very well," she said. "I'll attend the dinner."

Relief shone in both of her friends' eyes.

"Thank you," Felicity said. She seemed to hesitate before asking, "You'll bring Edward with you?"

Sophia couldn't very well go alone, and since the Fenmores didn't care for grand affairs, he was her best choice of companion. "Yes. But not as my fake fiancé."

Having to see Jack again would be bad enough without also trying to deceive him.

But when she spoke with Edward later, Sophia realized she wouldn't have to do so if she agreed to his proposal. She stared at him while trying to come to grips with what he'd just said. "You… You want to marry me? In truth?"

He gave her a frank look. "Lady Felicity and her sister gave me the idea."

Sophia blinked. "What they proposed, according to what I know, was for you and me to fake an engagement in the hope that Hawthorne would try and pursue me. I realize how ridiculous that sounds, but I suppose they think he'd get jealous or something and… Well, I told them I wouldn't do it."

"Because it would be wrong," Edward said.

Sophia nodded. "Exactly."

"But would it be so terribly wrong of you to actually consider me instead? As a genuine option?"

She shook her head. "You don't love me, Edward. Not in that way at least. Do you?"

He shrugged. "I love you in my own sort of way, Sophia. And as such, I do believe you and I could be happy together."

"But what about…" She waved her hand to avoid speaking the word.

"Desire?" he asked, studying her. When she gave a quick nod, he said, "In my opinion it's overrated. Of greater importance is how well we get along, and you and I have a shared history. Our values are similar. I know you, Sophia, and you know me."

"I suppose that's true."

There was a pause, and then he reached for her hand. "I realize your heart belongs to Hawthorne, but he has given you no reason to hope he'll ever be more to you than the brother of your dear friends."

This was true. In parting, he'd actually told her he expected to find her settled when he next saw her. The words had broken her heart and banished all hope. But to marry Edward?

She gazed at him, at the grave lines etched on his forehead and the firmness of his mouth. He'd chosen the same profession as his father and had just completed his eight-year-long education at seminary school a few months earlier. As such, he'd make an excellent catch for any gentlewoman from a good family. Especially once he got appointed to a parish.

Wanting only the best for him, Sophia could not ignore this fact and had to ask, "What about you, though? Are you certain you wish to throw away your chance of finding true love and happiness?"

He scoffed. "If I believed such things were within my reach, I'd chase them in a heartbeat. But as you know, life doesn't always give us what we wish for, which is not to say that you and I cannot have a wonderful life together. So I ask you, Sophia, to let me give you the security you need. I have no other attachments, and as such it would be an honor for me to make you my wife."

Sophia clasped his hand with all her might. He had proposed in the sort of practical way she should have expected from him. Devoid of passion but overflowing with endless fondness, he'd given her a better option than any woman in her position could have hoped for. It pained her to think he, too, might be walking away from the person he longed to spend the rest of his life with, but Sophia knew him well enough to understand he'd not do so unless he believed there was no other choice. To turn him down would be foolish. To suppose Jack would suddenly sweep her off her feet, more so.

And yet, marriage was not the sort of thing one ought to agree to on a whim. She needed time to clear her head – to think the matter through. "Will you let me sleep on it?"

He raised her hands to his lips and kissed them. "Of course."

By four o'clock the following morning, Sophia decided that 'sleeping on it' was a funny turn of phrase indeed. She'd not slept a wink, but she had managed to make up her mind.

If Jack needed to be persuaded to give her a chance, then she didn't want him. During his absence, she'd written him. Some might think it inappropriate for an unmarried woman to correspond with a bachelor, but the Fenmores had permitted it due to their longstanding friendship when she'd asked if it was alright. Jack, however, had not responded to any of her letters.

And Sophia had her pride. Chasing after a man who'd proven he had no interest in her was demeaning. She could do better and Edward was willing to give her exactly that – a comfortable life filled with friendship and affection.

And because of this - because she knew what she could expect from Edward and also because of how much she owed him and his parents - she pulled him aside immediately after breakfast and gave him her answer. "Yes, Edward. I will marry you."

Comfortably seated in the library, Jack enjoyed a pre-dinner drink with the gentleman suitors who'd been invited to vie for his sisters' hands. Lord, it was good to be back at Eastgate. He'd missed the sprawling estate much more than he'd realized. During his morning ride, he and his mount, Star, had savored a hard gallop, the chance to leap across fences and rivers, the ability to soar. Riding through Hyde Park was terribly dull by comparison.

Town also didn't permit him to hunt. One couldn't just shoot a duck swimming along the Serpentine and bring it home for supper. Tomorrow, however, he'd set out with the guests. They'd all expressed an interest in helping him catch a deer for the cook to prepare when he'd voiced the suggestion. The forest on the south side of the property would be an excellent spot for that. He knew it well, like the back of his hand. It was where he'd built his best forts as a child and also where he'd played his favorite games of hide and go seek with his sisters and the Fenmore children.

He paused on that thought as the memories flooded his brain, of laughter and mischief filling the air. Edward was the same age as he but had been the careful sort. If given the choice, he'd always preferred spending time with Jack's sisters who'd been more reserved on account of their being raised as young ladies. Sophia, on the other hand, had been entirely different – spirited and free from the restraint so often placed on people who worried about their appearances.

Jack smiled and took a sip of his brandy. She'd disliked sitting still on a blanket and making daisy chains. Even pall-mall had appeared to bore her, which was likely why she always whacked the ball as hard as she could with no attempt at all to make it roll through the appointed arches. Perhaps this was why she'd sought him out? Because she'd recognized in him a kindred spirit? When given the chance, she'd bombarded him with questions and comments, proving herself to be more precocious than most children her age. As such, he'd never really considered her youth. Nor had he paid much attention to the woman she'd been transforming into.

Until his father brought it up.

Jack tightened his grip on his glass as that one particular conversation came rushing back. It was what had caused him not only to leave but to stay away. Lord help him, he'd been angry. And determined to make sure he'd never have to rely on his father for anything ever again – not even his bloody inheritance.

Another sip of brandy slid down his throat. The bastard had threatened to withhold every penny if Jack did something reckless, like marry a woman unfit to hold a title. As if he'd had any notion of marrying anyone. The fact that his father had made an issue of it was preposterous.

He glanced at the man with whom he'd agreed to be civil for his sisters' sakes. They needed him now, but once they were married, Jack would go back to London where he could be free to indulge, much to his father's frustration. Jack grinned. With his investments providing him a comfortable income, his father no longer had the power to sway him in any way. Which was precisely how Jack liked it.

Still, in spite of their differences, Jack had to admit he owed his father one debt of gratitude. He'd brought Sophia's increased interest in him to his attention, offering Jack the chance to save her from an impossible dream by adding some much needed distance between them. Regrettably, the mixture of anger and frustration he'd experienced at the time had not led to the best sort of parting. In fact, his embarrassment over the words he'd spoken to her made him wary of running into her while he was here. But then again, it had been four years. Perhaps she'd forgotten?

"Shall we head on through to the parlor?" Papa inquired in a stiff voice. "It's almost six o'clock. The ladies will be down soon."

Jack stood, ready to do his duty regardless of the hostile air now swirling around him, and addressed the men nearest to him. "If you'll please follow me. It's time for us to greet Lady Turner and her daughters." He fell into step beside his father and led the way, arriving in the front-most parlor immediately before his mother and sisters made their entrance.

Closing the distance, he kissed each of their cheeks. He then stepped between his sisters and began to introduce them to the five men who'd be staying at Eastgate for the next three weeks. "You're already acquainted with the Earl of Cumberland, I believe. And this is Viscount Lambert… Mr. Madsen… Mr. Irving… and Mr. Dover."

"Enchanted," Mr. Dover murmured while gazing at Felicity in a manner that tempted Jack to hit him, never mind propriety or their friendship.

"It is my understanding that you are exceptional pianists," Viscount Lambert said, his eyes fixed on Kaitlin.

"And horsewomen," Mr. Irving added. "Perhaps we can go for a ride together tomorrow, if the weather permits."

"I'll come with you," Jack grumbled, only to receive a glare of disapproval from Felicity.

Really?

He glanced at his parents, who gestured for him to make himself scarce and allow his sisters some freedom to interact with the guests. For a second, he considered ignoring the request, only to get distracted when the butler arrived. He wasn't alone, but was escorting two people into the room and when he moved aside to give Jack a better view…

It was much like that one time when he'd landed

on his arse in a puddle after tripping over a fallen tree branch.

Air whooshed from his lungs. His heart seemed to stumble. Because there she was, exactly as he remembered her and yet so very different.

Jack blinked. When he'd last seen her he'd become aware that she was maturing, growing up and turning into a woman. Apparently this transition had since been completed. There were curves now where there had been straight lines before. High cheekbones had replaced the plump features she'd had during adolescence. Even her dark blonde hair looked more vibrant, her lips a deeper shade of rose. And then her gaze swept toward him, her bright green eyes shimmering with a mixture of joy, familiarity, and something else he couldn't quite place.

He started forward, drawn to her as if by some unseen force. Her smile deepened and his heart thumped hard against his chest.

"Sophia," Felicity said, intercepting Jack's path as she rushed to greet her friend. "I'm so glad you came."

"I did say I would," Sophia told her, and now Kaitlin had approached as well, blocking Sophia completely from Jack's line of sight. He frowned, but continued his approach, undaunted.

"And Mr. Fenmore," Felicity said. "I trust you are well?"

"Indeed," Edward replied. "Thank you for inviting us."

Jack reached the small group at the same time as his parents.

"Miss Fenmore," Mama said. "And Mr. Fenmore. You're most welcome."

Papa seconded the sentiment and then it was Jack's turn to offer his greetings. "It's good to see you again, Edward." He kept his gaze on his childhood friend for an extra second before allowing it to slide across to Sophia. "Miss Fenmore."

He wanted to say something else – to offer a compliment or…something. But as his eyes locked with hers, all sensible thought disappeared, and he could not for the life of him form a coherent sentence. So he just stood there like an imbecile – the most famous flirt in London, a reputed rake, reduced to a blithering fool on account of a woman.

A tight smile was all he could manage.

Sophia broke the gaze, effectively cutting him loose and sending him reeling as she gave her full attention to everyone else. "We're thrilled to be here. Especially since it gives us a chance to share our wonderful news with you directly."

Jack frowned. Why was she speaking as if she and Edward were one singular unit?

"You see," Sophia added with a glorious smile directed at Edward. "Mr. Fenmore has asked me to marry him, and I have accepted."

Exclamations of joy mixed with congratulations and squeals of excitement ensued, the cacophonous sound churning the air until it became a roar in Jack's ears. He stood as if paralyzed, not entirely certain of what he was feeling, though one distinct sensation did fill him, namely that of defeat.

"Come," Mama said. "Let me introduce the two of you to the rest of our guests."

Jack balled his hands into fists as Sophia and Edward moved off with his parents. He couldn't breathe. The air entering his lungs didn't seem to be working.

"Are you all right?" Kaitlin asked.

Somehow, in spite of the numbness, he managed a nod.

"You look a bit pale," Felicity said.

Jack turned his head toward her. "I need a drink."

"I'm so happy for Sophia and Edward," Felicity said, ignoring his comment. "It's about time they realized how perfect they are for each other."

Jack clenched his jaw. He couldn't wait to go hunting tomorrow. As of right now, he had an absurd need to shoot something while envisioning Edward's head.

"I quite agree," Kaitlin said as she and Felicity strolled away. "And winter weddings can be so romantic."

Jack gnashed his teeth and turned to the sideboard. A tall glass of brandy was in order. Right now. He poured himself a good measure and downed it, then poured himself another. Heat swept through him, easing some of the tension in his muscles.

As if by instinct, he glanced toward Sophia and Edward. They were conversing with Mr. Madsen and Mr. Dover while Cumberland, Irving, and Lambert kept Kaitlin and Felicity company.

Jack frowned. He took another sip of his drink and pondered the strong reaction he'd had upon learning Sophia and Edward were going to wed. It had felt like a blow to his skull, as if the predictable world he was used to had come crashing down around him. It felt…wrong. Sophia and Edward. He shook his head. His gut strained as if it wished to revolt against an unfavorable food. They couldn't be serious, could they?

And why the devil did he suddenly care so much about what Sophia decided to do with her life? What did it matter if she married Edward? It wasn't as if he wanted her for himself. Was it?

Of course not.

He might appreciate how stunning she suddenly looked – could not ignore the fact that she had grown into the sort of woman he might have considered pursuing if he'd been in London and she'd been an unhappy wife or widow. Instead she was here, in Oxfordshire, embodying the very essence of virginal purity. Regardless of her situation, Sophia Fenmore was not the sort of woman a self-respecting man dallied with unless he meant to marry her. Which was something Jack could not consider. In spite of his argument with his father, he respected his duty toward the title and as such, had resigned himself to the idea of eventually doing what most men in his position did and marrying for convenience alone.

For the first time in four years however, this very thought left a bitter taste in his mouth. It lingered as he followed the party into the dining room some moments later. He surveyed the place cards and instantly groaned. Of course he'd been seated beside her. Why the hell wouldn't he be?

2

CHAPTER TWO

IT TOOK tremendous effort on Sophia's part not to tremble as she slid into her seat at the table. More so when Jack lowered himself to the spot beside her. His nearness was like a jolt to her senses. Her heart had been racing madly since the moment she'd entered the parlor and seen him. Lord, her memory did not do him justice. Somehow, the last four years had carved away at his features to create a more chiseled appearance. It also seemed as if his shoulders had gotten broader, though that couldn't be quite right. Could it?

She dropped her gaze to the soup she'd been served and reached for her spoon with hesitant movements. It would be impolite not to eat, but she wasn't sure how to go about doing so when her stomach had been reduced to a tangled mess.

"I must confess," Jack murmured, the soft wool of

his jacket grazing the bare skin on her arm as he leaned in close. "Your announcement caught me off guard. Please forgive me and allow me to offer congratulations."

Awareness pulsed through her – the warmth of his nearness, the throaty sound of his voice thrumming around her, the enticing scent of sandalwood filling the air a heady concoction indeed. She swallowed and took a deep breath. Jack might have the power to make her feel more alive than anyone else, but he was a dream, a childish fantasy best forgotten. And she was engaged to Edward now. So she squared her shoulders and forced herself to meet his gaze.

Searching brown eyes pierced hers, almost making her catch her breath as her stomach curled inward. She took a moment to gather her strength. "Of course. I appreciate the sentiment."

A smile pulled at his lips. "You've changed, Sophia.

"Have I?"

He nodded, and then his gaze dipped lower, and something inside Sophia died. For four years she'd explained away the gossip about him, building excuses for him in her head, refusing to think him the rake scandal sheets painted him. And yet right now, with his attention directed toward her breasts, she had no trouble believing he was the worst sort of scoundrel.

Indeed, she wanted to toss her napkin in his face, or better yet, her wine.

The incident passed with swiftness – too quickly for anyone else to take note.

"I must say though, I never pictured you pairing up with Edward."

Coming on the heels of his blatant perusal, Sophia failed to hide the sudden flare of irritation his comment provoked. "And why is that?"

"It seems unnatural."

She stared at him. "What?"

"I mean, you're practically related."

"Except we're not."

He reached for his wine. "Come now, Sophia. You're like brother and sister."

"No more so than you and I," she hissed in annoyance.

"I have to disagree with you there. You and Edward were raised together. Like siblings." His lips quirked with seemingly innocent curiosity. "I mean, is that not how you've always viewed each other?"

Lord how she wanted to place her hands around his neck and strangle him. She tightened her grip on her spoon. "It is."

"So then, what difference does it make if you don't share the same birth parents?"

"I'd say it makes a world of difference when it comes to marriage," Sophia clipped. She turned away from him and started eating her soup while all manner of insults directed at Jack flew through her head. Why she'd ever fawned after him, she'd no idea. He was a cad.

"Do you perhaps find him desirable?"

The whispered words chipped away at her manners even as they swept over her shoulders and caused her to shiver. She cursed him for making her body respond with unwelcome pleasure. "Of course not. That would be…"

She stopped herself just in time and continued eating her soup.

"Odd?" Jack prompted with a low chuckle. "Impossible?"

Refusing to answer, she willed him to shut up and give his attention elsewhere. Or perhaps she should do so. Only Edward, who sat to her right, was presently engaged in conversation with Lady Turner.

"It does make one wonder about your reasoning," Jack added.

Sophia set her spoon aside, took a long sip of her wine, and swung her gaze back to the man she'd once dreamed of living happily ever after with. What on earth had she been thinking? "He and I have a history, my lord."

Irritation hardened his features. "You used to call me Jack."

"Mr. Fenmore and I understand each other," she added, deciding not to let his comment distract her from what she meant to say. "We care for one another. More to the point, he asked, in spite of my questionable parentage. It would have been downright foolish of me to turn him down. Especially since I love him."

This final statement seemed to render Jack mute. His eyes widened a fraction and then his lips parted as if he meant to respond. But then he just shook his head and turned his gaze away. To Sophia's consternation, it did not feel like the victory she'd hoped for, but rather like a defeat. It left her with a deflated sensation and a sense of unfathomable loss.

Getting through the rest of dinner was a chore. Constantly aware of the tempting woman who sat beside him, Jack wondered what the hell had possessed him to push her with all those improper inquiries. It wasn't like him to be rude or condescending, and yet he'd not be able stop the awful questions and comments from leaving his mouth. The need to provoke her had been too strong, and the manner in which she'd responded had only made it worse.

Fury had burned in her eyes, revealing the passionate nature that drew him to her when they'd been children. She'd always been a hoydenish imp with more of an interest in boyish pursuits, so he'd enjoyed her company whenever she'd come to visit since she was the only one who'd been willing to play in thick brush. Felicity, Kaitlin, and Edward had always preferred to keep their hair and clothes in order, and had kept each other company while Jack and Sophia burrowed their way through the hayloft in the stables. On the rare occasion when Edward didn't accompany her, Sophia would join him under a tree while his sisters picnicked with dolls. Not once had he thought of her as a girl. Hell, even when his father had suggested he and Sophia might end up together if he weren't careful, Jack had thought it laughable.

The realization confounded him as much as his response toward her. Because there was no denying the way his blood heated with each angry word she'd just spoken. And in the awful aftermath of this moment, he had to come to terms with a difficult truth.

Jack took a deep breath and allowed the idea of desiring Sophia Fenmore to settle. Damn, but he wanted her. Only she was now engaged to Edward – his friend.

The irony wasn't lost on him. God help him, it almost made him laugh. When he'd left, hadn't it been with the hope that Sophia would take a fancy to someone else?

Well, he hadn't expected that someone else to be Edward. Nor had he expected to regret with every fiber of his being his decision to stay away as long as he had. And yet just sitting beside her, inhaling her tempting scent of citrus and honey, was enough to make him wish he could stay right here beside her forever.

Ignoring his soup, he drank some more wine. At the rate which he consumed his drinks this evening, he'd be ten sheets to the wind in another half hour, a state he looked forward to with pleasure.

"I gather you chose to follow our plan after all," Felicity said after dinner. She'd drawn Sophia aside and led her toward a more private corner of the parlor where two chairs waited with a table between them. They sat.

"Not at all," Sophie said. "Edward proposed in earnest and I have accepted. The engagement is real."

"I...see."

Sophia studied her friend. "You sound disappointed."

"No, no." A smile was forced into place. "I'm happy for you. Truly I am. As long as this is what you want."

Unable to resist, Sophia allowed herself to seek out Jack. He stood on the opposite side of the room, glaring at her. She turned her attention back to Felicity. "It is."

"I'm glad." Felicity tilted her head. "I can't say the same for Jack though. Something tells me he's not happy with your engagement. So even if you no longer wish to attract his attention, I do believe you've managed it all the same."

Sophia pursed her lips. "Unfortunately, I fear you might be correct."

"Unfortunately?"

"Although I'll always be fond of him and the memories he helped create, my feelings for him aren't what they once were." How could they be when he wasn't the same carefree boy who'd been kind enough to mend the kite she'd made. The toy had gotten tangled in a tree and Jack had climbed up to fetch it. When she'd realized one side had gotten torn, she'd burst into tears. Jack had consoled her. Two days later, he'd brought the repaired kite to her at the vicarage.

Felicity smiled. "In that case, I'm all the happier for you since it would have pained me to watch you settle for one man while you still loved another."

"Indeed, if there's one thing I do know, it's that my love for Edward is real."

Felicity pressed her lips together. It was clear she had something else to add, but rather than say it, she smiled. "Have you settled on a date for the wedding yet?"

Sophia nodded. "Edward's father has suggested December twentieth, which allows us three Sundays for the banns. I have to get to work on the invitations tomorrow after church."

"I'm happy to help and Kaitlin is too, I believe."

"Thank you, but I'm sure you've enough to see to considering all the gentlemen hoping to gain your attention." Sophia swept the room with her gaze and managed to ignore Jack this time. "Do you have a preference yet?"

"I think it's too soon to tell."

When Sophia cut her a quizzical look on account of her breathy tone, she followed Felicity's line of sight to where Edward stood. He was keeping company with the earl and viscount.

"Either of those men would make an excellent match for you."

Felicity 's smile slipped before she managed to put it back into place. "Yes. I'm sure my parents agree."

Sophia shot another look at the men. Something in Felicity's tone was off. She almost sounded resigned. In a sad sort of way. But why should that be? Unless her friend's heart was otherwise engaged.

Sophia pondered this possibility before she said, "Would you rather consider someone else? Perhaps one of the gentlemen you met in London?"

Felicity gave her head a swift shake. "No. There is no one else."

"You're certain of this?"

"Of course." Felicity reached for Sophia's hand. "Come. Let's join the others."

Sophia stood and allowed Felicity to lead her over to where Kaitlin sat. Once seated, Sophia tried to pay attention to the ensuing conversation. It seemed Mr. Madsen was keen on cross pollinating fruit trees. Kaitlin listened to him with rapt attention while Felicity served Mr. Dover some tea and commented on her desire to try keeping bees.

Sophia did her best to focus on what was being said, only to find her thoughts wandering back to her recent conversation with Felicity. Her friend's assurances hadn't rung true, leaving Sophia with the distinct impression she had been lying, perhaps even to herself.

"Do you regret accepting my proposal?" Edward asked Sophia later as they headed home together in the carriage the Turners had lent them.

She turned to him in surprise. "No. Why on earth would I?"

His expression was hard to read in the dark but his words conveyed empathy. "I thought seeing him again might have caused you to change your mind."

"It has not. Quite the opposite, in fact."

"Sophia. " He spoke her name with the certainty of someone who knew her better than anyone else. "I know your feelings for Hawthorne run deep. Don't try to pretend they've suddenly vanished."

She fought the unhappy laughter that threatened

and managed a smile instead. "He's not how I remember him and I have changed as well. Besides, there was never any chance of our ending up together."

"Perhaps not," he agreed and reached for her hand. He gave it a gentle squeeze. "But that doesn't mean you aren't affected by having even the slimmest possibility removed."

"I might have been," she said, "if there weren't so many differences between us. You'll have to forgive me, Edward, but right now the thing that upsets me most is realizing how much we've grown apart." So much so she wondered if she could even call Jack her friend anymore. He'd unnerved her and thrown her off balance tonight, riled her until she'd wanted to scream. But he'd also made her want something she knew she had to resist.

"I'm just thinking…"

When Edward didn't elaborate, Sophia asked, "What?"

His hold on her hand tightened. "You deserve to experience passion, Sophia, which is something I think we can both admit you and I will never find with each other. So if the opportunity were to arise and…and you wanted to steal a moment for yourself, I wouldn't begrudge you."

Shocked by his implication, Sophia snatched her hand away from his and turned more fully toward him. "Are you suggesting I have an affair? That I become another of Jack's conquests?"

"No. What I'm suggesting is that you should do what feels right for you, provided you don't embarrass me in the process."

Sophia turned her gaze toward the carriage window, only to be faced by her own reflection. The sad expression of the woman staring back at her only made her unhappier. "I cannot believe we're having this conversation."

He sighed, the sound so achingly wretched it nearly brought tears to her eyes. "You deserve to know what it means to desire someone and to feel desire in return. I've had my own experiences and I know full well what I'm giving up. But you don't."

She jerked around and stared at him. "Surely desire will come if we're willing to try?"

He shook his head. "No, Sophia. Desire doesn't grow in the way love does. It's either there or it isn't, right from the start, a magnetic pull instilling in you a basic need to copulate. The luckiest people in the world are those who have both love and desire, although if one must choose, love is the better option because it is sure to last, while desire may fade with time. I know you love me as I love you, but I also know with equal certainty that you will never feel desire for me."

Indeed she would not. The very idea of climbing into bed with Edward was, as Jack had said, unnatural. And yet she would do it however many times she had to in order for them to conceive. Not the most romantic view of what married life promised to hold. She found she looked forward to it with dread. And with anger directed at Jack for ruining something that would have worked out so well had he not made her yearn for more than what she was permitted to have.

With his hands in his pockets and his posture rigid, Jack stood near the library window and glared at the landscape beyond. With only the fire burning behind him and three oil lamps scattered about the room, he could see the dark outline of the tree line where the forest began. A nerve ticked at the edge of his jaw. His brain felt like it had been dislodged. In fact, his skull hurt like blazes. Most likely from all the drink he'd poured down his throat that evening. Unfortunately, its soothing effect had faded hours ago without leading to the carefree state of drunken bliss he'd hoped for. Instead he felt exhausted, slightly unwell, and more irritated than when Sophia had first arrived and he'd learned of her engagement.

His jaw tightened. Why the hell should he care who she married? In fact, he ought to be thrilled on her behalf. In spite of the way in which he'd teased her – mocked her rather – for choosing Edward, he was a good match for her. Jack scowled at his reflection in the glass as he recalled the things he'd said. *It seems unnatural. I mean, you're practically related. Come now, Sophia. You're like brother and sister.*

He winced. If one didn't know any better, one might suppose he was jealous.

Which he wasn't.

The preposterous notion almost caused him to laugh. He scrubbed one hand across his jaw and muttered a curse.

"So this is where you're hiding." Felicity's voice made him turn. She stood in the doorway with Kaitlin directly behind her. "Just so you know, Cumberland won the game."

Jack nodded. He'd suggested billiards after Sophia and Edward's departure, but with his mind elsewhere, he'd played worse than ever before and had quietly snuck from the room in search of solace. "Have he and the rest of the guests retired then?"

"Most of them." Felicity and Kaitlin stepped into the room and shut the door. "When we left, Cumberland and Lambert were smoking cheroots on the terrace." Felicity wrinkled her nose and made her approach. "You've been a bit odd all evening, so we thought it best to check on you."

"I'm fine."

"Were you not pleased to see Sophia and Edward again?" Kaitlin asked.

Jack curled his fingers, digging his nails into his palms. "You could have told me they were coming."

"We wanted it to be a surprise," Felicity said.

The humorless laughter that threatened earlier rose from his throat with gruffness. "It certainly was that."

"I must confess, their intention to wed got the best of us too," Kaitlin said. "But I for one am happy for them."

Jack stared at his sister. He told himself not to comment. And yet, the words slipped out all the same. "They're completely ill-suited."

"I wouldn't say that," Felicity countered. "They've grown up together which means they already have a strong bond. This alone should make their marriage an easy one."

He snorted and turned away in an effort to hide his sudden anger. "I ought to get myself to bed." What he meant was he needed to flee, rid himself of his sisters who clearly wished to discuss a subject he hoped to avoid.

"Honestly, Jack. I don't know why you're in such a mood," Felicity commented. "It's as if you begrudge them their happiness, which doesn't really seem fair. I mean, they're your friends. You ought to be thrilled on their behalf. Especially for Sophia whose prospects have never been much to speak of."

"I'm not suggesting she could do better, but for her to marry Edward of all people is just so...so..."

"What?" Kaitlin asked as if what he said next would change the world.

He swung back toward them and stared at their expectant faces. Eventually, he shook his head. "Nothing. I'm sure I just need to get used to the idea of them as husband and wife."

"Is that all?" Felicity asked.

"Of course." He started for the door. "What else could it possibly be? If you'll excuse me, I'm going to try and get some sleep. Good night."

"You know," Kaitlin said, her gentle voice catching him right before he managed to leave the room. "They're not married yet."

He glanced over his shoulder. "What the hell is that supposed to mean?"

Kaitlin shrugged. "Nothing. Forget I said anything."

Jack scowled and quit their presence with a clipped stride. His sister's words had not been *nothing,* and the chance of him forgetting them was as likely as him ignoring his sudden and most inconvenient attraction toward Sophia Fenmore.

CHAPTER THREE

THE CHRISTMAS SEASON was always busy at the vicarage, and with December approaching fast, there was much to be done. Pine needed to be gathered for the church decorations, biscuits had to be baked, bags of chestnuts filled, and jams readied for the baskets going to poor families in the area. Each would also receive a smoked hen this year, thanks to Sophia's charity efforts.

She selected one of the hens from the crate in which it had been delivered, wrapped it in brown paper, and tied a red ribbon around it. After finishing off with a neat bow she placed the hen in a basket. A tin filled with ginger biscuits and short-bread was placed on top along with a jar filled with cherry preserves. The bag of chestnuts, bearing a label that read, *to the Richmond Family with best wishes for a happy holiday season*, was added last, even though Sophia wasn't sure they'd be able to read it.

"Here's the final tray of biscuits for you," Mrs. Fenmore said as she bustled into the pantry where Sophia worked. She set the tray on an empty shelf. "All I have to do now is roast the last chestnuts. How are you coming along in here, my dear?"

"Pretty well. I'm thinking I ought to start distributing the baskets that are ready. The remaining hens can be stored in the shed until later."

"I agree. With the temperatures below freezing, they'll keep best out there." Mrs. Fenmore smiled. "Once we've gotten this done, we can start planning for your big day. I'm thinking a visit to Audrey's Couture on High Street might be in order. The seamstresses there did an excellent job on Amy Larkin's wedding gown in the spring."

"Thank you," Sophia said, a little overcome by her adoptive mother's enthusiasm, "but I can easily modify one of the dresses I already own. There's really no need to purchase a new one."

"Pish. You're like the daughter I never had and you're marrying my only child. Of course I plan to help make the day as special for you as possible, starting with the gown. I won't take no for an answer." She shook her finger at Sophia before she turned away and disappeared back to the kitchen.

Air left Sophia's lungs on a long exhalation. She very much feared Mr. Fenmore and his wife were far more excited about the upcoming wedding than she or Edward would ever be. And this bothered her. More so because thoughts of Jack kept filling her head. No matter how much she tried, she could not forget the effect his nearness had wrought on her during dinner at Eastgate Abbey five days earlier. He'd not been kind, but that didn't seem to stop her treacherous body from wanting. A flutter caught hold of her heart, increasing in strength as the conversation she'd had with Edward later resurfaced.

She gripped the edge of the counter and stared at the baskets she had completed that morning, which now totaled six. Although she would never allow herself be swept away by Jack while she was engaged to another, having Edward's permission had caused all manner of indecent thoughts to swamp her brain. They'd invaded her dreams, leaving her breathless when she woke.

"Madness."

All she could do was pray it would stop once she spoke her vows. Jack wasn't her friend anymore. Perhaps he never had been. Maybe all she'd ever been to him was a pesky child. She was no longer sure. Everything had become such a muddle. She'd thought she understood him once, but then… Then she'd learned of all the women sauntering in and out of his life, and while she'd not believed a word until it had been confirmed, she'd been jealous. Mostly because she'd known deep inside that she would never stand a chance of gaining his notice. Not in the way she wanted.

She still hadn't. All she was to him now was a lost opportunity. He didn't want a future with her, so even if he cared for her in some small way on account of their shared history, anything more than a bit of fun would always be impossible.

And why was she even having these foolish musings?

Perhaps because Kaitlin and Felicity had called on her two days ago to inform her that Jack had been in a constant state of pique ever since that dinner. Because they believed she was to blame. According to what they'd said, he'd made a hash of the hunt he'd invited the guests to attend, returning empty handed after missing three times and frightening off the prey. From there, things had apparently gotten worse. He'd accused Mr. Madsen of cheating at cards, had complained about the food not being up to par – resulting in a massive row below stairs – and insisted Eastgate was a damp and dreary place he ought to have stayed away from.

"He's like a dark cloud hanging over the house and spoiling everyone's fun," Kaitlin complained.

"I don't understand," Sophia said. "Jack was always so sporting. He used to be the one who made everyone laugh." He'd always cheered her up. When she'd scraped her knee, he'd joked about her looking like a hardened soldier, upon which he'd offered a sweet.

Felicity harrumphed. "I don't believe he's ever been denied anything before, and now he's not just being denied but realizing he can't have something he never knew he wanted."

"Whatever are you going on about?" Sophia asked.

Kaitlin sighed. "You're driving our brother round the bend, Sophia."

"But I'm not even there," she'd protested.

Sophia shook her head to free her mind from the words she'd exchanged with her friends and started bundling up. It was best if she thought of something else, like the baskets she had to deliver.

Grabbing two of them, she set off for the Bakers and the Walkers since they lived closest. Her breath fogged the air, but the fur-trimmed winter hat she wore along with a pair of thick woolen mittens helped keep her warm. Both families showed appreciation for her visit. They invited her in and offered her tea, then chatted with her for a good fifteen minutes until she took her leave.

When she returned to the vicarage, she glanced at the hallway clock. It was almost two in the afternoon. If she hurried, she could reach the Richmonds by half past and the Scotts by three, leaving her just enough time to make the final deliveries of the day before it got dark.

Collecting the baskets, she headed back out, and made her way toward the northbound road at a brisk pace. Grey clouds were beginning to gather, but the Richmonds' cottage was only one and a half miles away, the home belonging to the Scotts just slightly farther, provided she cut across some of the fields. No doubt she'd return before the weather grew hostile.

"Miss Fenmore," Mrs. Richmond proclaimed when Sophia showed up at her first destination. "Please do come in."

Sophia smiled and stepped across the threshold.

"I'm sorry we've not much to offer," Mrs. Richmond said while cradling her youngest son on her hip. "We ran out of tea yesterday and with the two eldest sick with a nasty cold and the roof in need of repair, neither my husband nor I have managed to get to Town since Wednesday."

"No need for apologies," Sophia said. She followed Mrs. Richmond into the parlor where one of her younger daughters busied herself with some mending. "What's wrong with your roof exactly?"

Mrs. Richmond sighed. "Looks like some of the rafters have rotted through. When it rained a few days ago, part of it collapsed. Mr. Richmond's up there now attempting to fix it with Lord Hawthorne's help. They're in the attic."

Sophia froze. Jack was here? She'd not noticed a horse or a carriage when she' arrived, but maybe they'd been taken around to the back. She wondered how to proceed and quickly made her decision. Meeting Jack would be awkward, so it was best if she could avoid him completely.

She set her basket on a table. "I hope this will help the situation in some small way, Mrs. Richmond, and please don't trouble yourself about the tea. I don't have time to stay anyway since I've yet to reach the Scotts' and run two more errands before it gets dark." She paused, then said, "I'll send some honey over tomorrow along with some lemons. That ought to help your children get better."

"Thank you ever so much," Mrs. Richmond said, her voice cracking. "You're so very kind."

Sophia smiled and turned for the door, reaching it just in time to hear footsteps on the stairs. She hastened across the tiny hallway, desperate to escape before Jack found her. The basket she held for the Scotts caught the railing. A voice, Mr. Richmond's no doubt, said, "I hardly know how to thank you, my lord."

"I'm sure I can think of something."

Sophia recognized Jack's low timbre and frowned. If he meant to take advantage of these people she'd—

"Help me fix the broken axel on my carriage and I'd say we're even."

Sophia took a step back. A pair of muddied clogs and a pair of expensive boots came into view. Her stomach twisted with the awareness of having misjudged Jack. He'd taken time out of his day to help mend a broken roof, and all he wanted as payment was help in return.

Nevertheless, she reached for the handle behind her. She needed to think, get her muddled thoughts in order. The way he'd acted toward her at Eastgate – the things he'd said - had clearly skewed her opinion of him. Which wasn't really fair since he'd always been a good person. She'd loved him for a good reason. And yet, she had no wish to encounter him now, so she turned, hoping to rush out the door before he saw her.

"Sophia?"

She muttered a curse and turned, pasting a smile on her face as she did so. "Lord Hawthorne. What a coincidence."

His gaze, dark and intense, captured hers. "I prefer to think of it as serendipitous."

Before she had a chance to comment, he told Mr. Richmond, "I shall return tomorrow with the wood and shingles you need. The temporary boards and support posts we've just installed should hold until then, even if it rains."

Mr. Richmond thanked him and gave Sophia his full attention. "Miss Fenmore. You're most welcome."

"She brought us a lovely holiday basket," Mrs.

Richmond told her husband from the parlor doorway.

"Our thanks," Mr. Richmond said. "Your generosity knows no bounds, does it, Miss Fenmore?"

Flustered, Sophia averted her gaze as heat crept into her cheeks. "I'll stop by again tomorrow as promised. Good bye, Mrs. Richmond. Mr. Richmond. Lord Hawthorne."

She accidentally stubbed her toes on the door and tripped in her haste to be gone. Once outside, she took a deep breath and forced her legs into motion. If she hurried, then maybe, just maybe, she might be lucky enough to disappear from sight before Jack emerged from the cottage.

Clutching the basket meant for the Scotts, she broke into a near run, desperate to get away before he saw the direction in which she headed.

Why she was so intent on escape, she wasn't quite sure. Everything she'd been feeling for six long years, since she'd first become aware of the love she harbored for Jack, was spinning around inside her. Before his return last week, she'd managed to suppress it, to push it down and convince herself it was just a silly infatuation. That it no longer existed.

But she was older now and the response he'd managed to coax from her during dinner terrified her. In spite of his words and the anger they'd caused, he'd made her want something new and different – something that made her long for his touch. The sensation was stronger than the innocent admiration she'd had for him as a child, more powerful than the love he'd instilled in her heart as she'd grown older, a force so intense it threatened to draw her to him no matter how much she resisted the pull.

So she rushed across the road and into the field before he could catch her, tripping and stumbling due to the steep descent.

"Sophia!"

Her breath hitched but she kept going, adding distance as fast as she could even though the pounding of hooves rumbled through the ground to signal his rapid approach.

Her foot slipped and she suddenly fell, skidding through the dry grass until she lost her balance completely.

"Hell and damnation." Jack landed beside her, the reins from his horse caught in one hand as he crouched down and reached for her elbow. Warm fingers curled around her arm. "Are you all right?"

She blinked, slightly dazed, and glanced at him.

A frown of concern marred his forehead.

"I'm fine." She yanked herself free and pushed to her feet, ignoring the hand he offered as much as the pleasure she'd found in his touch.

He straightened and as he did so, his frown deepened. When he spoke, his voice was hard, accusatory. "Why would you run from me like that?"

"I wasn't running from you," she lied, unwilling to try and explain her confusion or the conflicting emotions he forced upon her. It would be a futile effort when she barely understood them herself, and besides, she had no wish to reveal the power he held over her.

"No?" He glared at her as if she'd done something wrong when he was the one who hadn't written or come to visit for nearly four years.

Setting her jaw she grabbed her basket and recommenced walking. "I've deliveries to make before it gets dark. Judging from those clouds, it may even start to snow soon. *That* is why I was hurrying. My actions have nothing to do with you."

"So you're not trying to avoid me?" he asked, falling into step beside her while pulling his horse along with him.

"Why would I do that?"

There was a pause and then he said, "I thought perhaps my comments the other evening about you and Edward upset you. I'm sorry if that's the case but my sisters didn't warn me. They never even told me you'd be there. So I was surprised, that's all."

She glanced at him, at his tight expression. "You spoke your mind as usual and since that's something I've always liked about you, it would be wrong of me to find fault with it when your view disagrees with mine."

"I just don't see you being happy with him, Sophia." He looked her squarely in the eye for a second before turning his gaze away, but it was enough for her to glimpse the incomprehension he felt with regard to her engagement.

"Why not?" she asked. "We've known each other most of our lives, have shared every up and down, and understand each other well enough for me to be certain we'll always be able to solve our differences."

"That's not enough."

"How can you say that?" Once again his comment poked at her doubts and put her on edge. "Edward is easy for me to talk to. With him I always know what to expect."

"In other words," Jack remarked, "he's the safe option."

"No," she told him hotly, "he is the only option. No one else has ever asked and I cannot afford to sit and wait for them to do so."

"And because of this, you've decided to settle."

God, how she wanted to swing her basket at his head, throw its contents at him until he ducked away or better yet, ran. "Edward's a good man, Jack. The very finest, in fact. And as his friend – as *my* friend – your lack of support confounds me."

"Maybe it is the very friendship you speak of that prompts me to say what no one else will, Sophia.

You and Edward are wrong for each other. You will always be wrong for each other." His voice grew in strength, his eyes flashing with stormy emotion while they both increased their speed as if each meant to outpace the other. "No matter how easy or practical marrying him may be, he will never be able to give you what you need just as you will never give him what he needs."

She halted so she could glare at him properly. "What are you talking about?"

"You seek adventure while he's always been the careful sort. As children, you were the one who suggested building a raft for the lake. Edward tried to talk you out of it because he believed a raft built by children would lead to disaster."

In the end, Jack had helped her fulfill her vision while Edward, Felicity, and Kaitlin busied themselves with a game of cards. She placed her free hand on her hip. "There's nothing wrong with being cautious. In fact, I'd say it will serve me well if my husband is able to temper my spirit a little."

"Edward won't temper it, though," Jack told her. "That's the problem. He'll stifle you completely."

She shook her head. "You're mistaken."

"Am I?" When she didn't comment, he said, "You always liked to climb trees and build forts. He didn't. When you suggested tying a rope to one of the branches hanging over the lake so we could launch ourselves into the water, he said it was time to go home. He is serious while you are not. If given the choice, he would rather stay home reading a book than join in a horse race or…or visit a tavern with friends."

"There's nothing wrong with being responsible."

"Of course not, but Edward is like an octogenarian in a young body. He's always been that way. There's no playfulness about him the way there is with you."

"Perhaps not," she agreed. It was true Edward was stuffy and always more serious than she could ever be. "But he is dependable, which is more than I can say about you."

"What?"

"How many times did I write you over the last four years?" When he opened his mouth she said, "Once a week, Jack. And you never wrote back. Never mind the fact that you stayed away. Not once did you come to visit even though London is not so terribly far."

"You never came to see me either," he countered.

"How could I? An unmarried woman does not go to London alone. To suggest that doing so was even an option is utter nonsense as well you know. But at least I wrote." She pressed her fist to her breast and leaned toward him. "I wrote you, Jack. And you didn't respond."

CHAPTER FOUR

GUILT DUG into Jack and clawed at his conscience. She wasn't wrong. He'd made no effort to keep in touch. Quite the contrary. At first, because he'd hoped to discourage her growing interest in him. Later, because he hadn't known what to say. Time had made any answer he might pen feel awkward.

So he looked at her now, at the accusation in her eyes. There was hurt there as well, which was what truly pained him. He'd never intended to break her heart or crush her spirit. It occurred to him now he might have done so.

With Star's reins clasped loosely in his hand, he said, "Forgive me, Sophia. The last four years have been busy for me."

Her eyes hardened, holding his for a moment more before she gave a disdainful snort and started walking away from him once more. "Yes. I know. It's a wonder you found the time to come here at all what with all the women climbing in and out of your bed."

That she would address his love life so openly shocked him. He stared after her, unable to find the right words.

"You may disparage Edward for being a bore," she added, "but at least he's a gentleman. I've never had cause to question his moral compass, though I can't say the same about you."

The sudden fury she stirred in him caught him utterly unawares. Before he could think, he'd caught up with her, snatched her by the arm, and spun her toward him. "You know nothing of my situation, Sophia. How dare you judge me?"

"I judge you with the knowledge I have in my possession. According to what I have read, you are a flirt, a seducer of women, a rake of the highest—"

"Careful," he gritted. His hold on her tightened and he took some pleasure, perverse as it was, in watching her eyes widen with apprehension. Satisfaction coursed through him, bonding with the tension she'd pushed through his veins. "I am not the heartless bastard you wish to paint me, Sophia."

She raised her chin, defiance evident in her expression. "Release me."

Still reeling from the accusation she'd spoken against him, he did as she asked without hesitation.

The words - the pure contempt with which she'd said them - hurt like nothing else.

Worse was the realization that he had caused this. Four years ago he'd set out for two distinct reasons: to get away from his father and to make Sophia lose interest in him. And he'd succeeded. But having to face the woman who'd once gazed upon him with awe and adoration when she'd been a child only to realize he'd lost her trust and respect was like a thousand lashes across his heart. It felt as though he'd been cut wide open and was having salt pushed into his wound.

This was a situation of his own making, and he had no one to blame but himself.

Acknowledging this, he chose to say nothing more on the matter. Instead, he gestured toward her basket. "Allow me to carry that for you."

She glanced in the direction she'd been heading and spoke without looking at him. "I think it might be best if you went home. I'd rather walk alone."

An awful sense of loss swept through him. His throat tightened in response and it became hard to breathe. She was pushing him away and he sensed that if he let her, it would mark the end of their friendship. No matter how much he'd wronged her, regardless of the mistakes he'd made where she was concerned, he could not let her ruin the one thing he valued above all else: knowing she'd be there, no matter what – a constant in the madness of his life.

He stilled on that thought. Was this why her engagement to Edward upset him so? Because it heralded change? Because his childhood friend was moving on without him? Not Edward, but her. And if so, had he not taken her for granted, to suppose she wouldn't – to imagine he could return at any time and pick up where they'd left off? That everything would stay the same?

His chest ached as he realized he'd put the most important relationship he'd ever had in jeopardy. She was his best friend. Sophia, not Edward. *She'd* been the one with whom he'd always felt the strongest connection, the boisterous girl with whom he'd gazed up at the sky in search of peculiar cloud formations, the imp who'd clapped with glee when he'd shown her a new magic trick he'd learned, and the one person he'd always looked forward to seeing above all others whenever he'd come home from school on holiday.

She mattered to him more than anyone else and rather than give her respect, he'd ignored her out of fear - fear he might not be as indifferent to her as he'd told his father, fear he'd want an impossible future, fear he would end up spending the rest of his life with someone who wasn't Sophia.

"I can't let you walk alone," he said, more determined than ever to stay by her side. "It wouldn't be right."

Her reluctance was evident in the flattening of

her mouth. She sighed. "Fine. As long as we don't have to talk. My head hurts from all the arguing."

He rather agreed. And since he'd always found pleasure in sharing silences with her when he'd been younger, he took no issue with her request. In fact, he was glad of it, since it gave him a chance to gather his thoughts. And there were a lot of thoughts, all of them buzzing about his brain while he trudged along beside her, leading Star by the reins.

Eventually, having circled back to the comment she'd made about him being a rake, he decided he had to say something. "I never ruined anyone, you know."

"Sorry?"

It sounded like she'd been deep in thought. Her quizzical expression confirmed this. So he added, "That's what rakes do. They're scoundrels who take advantage of naïve young girls, luring them astray and then abandoning them to the repercussions. I don't do that, Sophia. I only flirt a little with some of the debutantes, mostly to boost their confidence. The...um...the women I've...um...entertained, were either widowed or..."

"Or?" she asked when he paused to consider his words.

This was a delicate subject. It wasn't the sort of thing a gentleman broached with an unmarried woman. And yet, he sensed being honest would help reduce the rift between them. So he bolstered himself against the shame of addressing such personal details of his life with her, told himself he had to for the sake of their friendship, and said, "There are unmarried women who seek to improve their situation by exchanging favors of an intimate nature."

"You refer to whores?"

He choked on the air he was breathing. "Not entirely. Some are ballerinas, opera singers, and actresses. Women who wish to be independent while still enjoying the company of men."

She cut him a look and raised an eyebrow as they reached the opposite side of the field. The Scotts' cottage came into view roughly one hundred yards away. They'd be there soon, which was good since the clouds that had been in the sky when he'd left Eastgate earlier had darkened.

"From what I understand there were married women too. Other men's wives?"

He swallowed. "Yes. Well. I can't deny my dalliances with Lady Preston or Lady Laxonberry."

Sophia shook her head and scoffed. "And yet you seek my approval. Well, you shan't have it, Jack. What you've done is wrong."

Jack was sure the church would agree. But things weren't always as black and white as Sophia wished to make them. "One should be wary of judging others as swiftly as you are inclined to do. Have you ever met these women or their husbands? Do you know a single thing about them?"

"Of course not."

He grabbed her elbow and drew her to a halt. "Sophia, you know me."

"I believe I used to, but now…" She shook her head and stared in the direction they were headed.

Curling his fingers more securely around her arm, Jack held onto her as though she were his lifeline. It was vital he change her opinion of him. For the first time ever, he sensed his entire existence might be at stake if he failed to do so. "Lady Preston is five-and-thirty years of age."

"I do not wish to know the sordid details of your debauchery." Sophia yanked on her arm, but Jack held her in place.

"When she was but eighteen years old, her parents married her off to Viscount Preston, a lecherous man forty-five years her senior with whom she has since been forced to share her bed." Noting the wide-eyed look of shock in Sophia's eyes, Jack continued. "As for Lady Laxonberry, her husband is a notorious brute. As someone who has seen her unclothed, I can vouch for that. Her body is always marked with bruises."

"Good lord."

"Both women sought comfort in my arms. I'll not apologize for offering them a moment's escape from an otherwise horrid life. My only regret is getting found out. Both women suffered because of it, especially Lady Laxonberry."

"I'm sorry. I didn't know."

"No, but you were very keen to make assumptions and think the worst. Weren't you?"

"Forgive me, Jack."

He loosened his grip on her arm, then released her so she could recommence walking. A frown pulled at his forehead as he fell into step beside her. "I wish you had confronted me sooner. Instead, you try to avoid me."

He saw her cheeks flame even as she said, "I already told you. I'm just in a hurry, that's all. My leaving the Richmonds' with haste had nothing to do with you in the least."

He didn't believe her. She'd been on the attack since he'd caught up with her fifteen minutes ago, pushing and prodding, provoking a fight as if he were a threat and words were her weapons.

He lost his chance to say as much when they arrived at the Scotts' front door.

Sophia knocked and when Mrs. Scott arrived, she offered her the basket.

"Thank you, Miss Fenmore." Perpetual sadness clung to Mrs. Scott's eyes. The deep grooves set in her face a stark reminder of all she'd lost. "Won't you come in?"

Jack's heart clenched in memory of the frozen lake her boys had succumbed to. The youngest lad had fallen through and the oldest had tried to save his brother. Both had eventually perished.

"I'm afraid we can't stay," Sophia said. She offered a smile and placed one had on Mrs. Scott's arm. "Please give our regards to your husband."

"Yes," Mrs. Scott said. She pressed her lips together and nodded. "We'll see you at church on Sunday."

"Come," Jack said once he and Sophia had finished taking their leave of Mrs. Scott. "I don't like the way the wind's picking up now and those clouds look mighty threatening."

She glanced at the sky and frowned. "Do you think it will start to snow before we get back to Town?"

"It might, which is why I suggest we hurry." He led Star onto the road and steadied him. "Allow me to help you up."

She stared at him. "If I ride, then what will you do?"

"We'll ride together." When she drew back, he waved with increased impatience. "Time is of the essence, Sophia, so please put aside whatever grudge you're still holding toward me and get on the horse."

"I really don't think this is a good idea." She seemed to consider the road. "I'm perfectly fine walking. It won't take more than forty-five minutes for me to reach home."

Something wet landed on Jack's forehead. "During which you may catch your death."

"I've never been sick in my life," she argued, and promptly set off at a brisk pace.

Jack muttered a curse and followed. Lord, how he wanted to strangle her right now. Tempering himself, he did his best to convey calm and reason as he said, "Edward will never forgive me if I don't see you home safely."

"And so you shall," she quipped. "On foot."

"Stubborn chit," he grumbled, and suddenly grinned when he noticed her smile. Unable to resist, he drew a bit closer to her and gave her shoulder a nudge. "Impossible female."

"Impudent rogue," she countered, all seriousness in spite of her twinkling eyes.

Jack felt himself relax for the first time since their reunion. This was what he'd always enjoyed about her – this teasing manner and fearless wit.

Additional rain, not snow, began to fall. Sophia seemed not to notice as she asked, "So who do you think your sisters will marry?"

The unexpected question threw him. "I haven't really considered. And I'm not sure they have either."

She was quiet for a moment. The wind grew stronger and Jack considered ordering her onto the horse. But then she distracted him by saying, "I fear Felicity's heart may already be engaged."

This, Jack hadn't expected. "Has she said something to you?"

"No. But I have a feeling she is resigning herself to what you and your parents expect of her."

He didn't like that idea at all. "Of course I want both my sisters to marry, but I also wish them happy. My parents do too, I'm sure. For my own part, I can only say that if Felicity has formed some sort of attachment with a gentleman of her own choosing, she need only come to me and ask for my blessing."

"Unless she doesn't think you'd approve," Sophia suggested.

"That doesn't mean I wouldn't listen." He shook his head. When had it come to this? How was it that everyone in his life thought the worst of him? Sophia believed him a scoundrel, Felicity an oppressor of sorts. Yet all he wanted – all he had ever wanted – was to try and ensure their happiness by keeping them safe. His sisters by helping them both make favorable matches, Sophia by crushing whatever romantic notions she might have started having of him lest she think they could have a future.

Four years ago, he'd had no interest in marriage. Hell, he'd barely known he had a heart or that it could ever belong to one single woman. So when his father had warned him away from Sophia with threats of cutting him off, he'd left for her sake as much as his own. Driven by a fierce desire to hurt his father in return, he'd entered into one liaison after another with every intention of adding a smudge here and there to the otherwise pristine family name.

He grimaced as he recalled the conversation that had led to the rift between them.

"Sophia Fenmore is growing up," Papa had said, "and I fear she's becoming aware of you in ways she wasn't before."

"What are you getting at?" Jack asked.

"Be careful, Jack. A woman like her can never be more than your mistress and—"

"You insult her with what you are saying, and you insult me by supposing I'd ever cross the bonds of friendship between us."

"You cannot tell me you're blind to her interest. Don't think I haven't noticed her seeking you out with greater frequency than when she was younger. My fear, Jack, is that she no longer comes here to see your sisters, but purely in the hope of gaining your notice."

"What you suggest is ridiculous. She's but a child."

"A child on the cusp of womanhood, Jack. Surely you must have noticed."

To Jack's complete and utter amazement, it wasn't something he had considered until that exact conversation. And then he'd not been able to think of anything else. So he'd called on her and had, during his visit, discerned that he must be both daft and blind. Because Sophia was not only turning into a woman, but a shockingly tempting one too, even though her feminine allure then was nothing compared to what it was now.

When he'd left, he'd had to acknowledge that their youth was over, that the casual friendship they'd had in their childhood would never be what it once was. They were now man and woman, and as this realization cemented itself, he'd felt his whole world slide sideways.

It hadn't helped matters when he'd returned to find his father waiting. Demands for Jack to stay away from Sophia henceforth had followed and Jack had called him unreasonable; the final threat had been issued. So he'd done the only thing he'd been able to think of in order to solve the problem.

He'd run.

From his father and from Sophia.

"I think we need to hurry," Sophia's voice jolted him out of his reverie.

A harsh gust of air caught the edge of his great-coat and pushed him into Star. Sophia drew her cloak around herself and bowed her head to the wind. Jack cast a glance at the swaying trees in the distance as more rain started to fall.

Damn!

Aware of the danger they faced if they got caught in a storm, he rounded on Sophia, placed his hands on her waist, and hoisted her onto Star. She gave a startled squeal which he ignored as he swung himself up behind her. He'd tried to do as she asked, but he would not risk her health for any reason. She could argue with him over it as much as she liked later. For now, he meant to see her returned to the vicarage before she got soaked through.

5

CHAPTER FIVE

IT WASN'T long before the clouds burst open and freezing rain descended upon them in torrents. At her back, Sophia could feel the warmth of Jack's chest pressing against her as he forced his horse into a hard gallop. Flecks of ice flew in her face, making her duck her head against the harsh wind while praying Jack would lead them home safely. Holding her steady between his arms, he leaned into the storm.

She'd not been prepared for this sort of thing, had not even sat in a saddle since she was fourteen, possibly younger. Yet here she was now, riding astride with her skirts hitched up around her legs and with Jack's thighs bracing hers. It was completely improper – scandalous in the extreme – and all she could think was, *at least it's winter rather than summer and my legs are covered in thick wool stockings.*

A blast of air whipped across the country road, swirling ice and rain in her face. The horse skidded and slid while Jack cursed. Sophia felt his entire body draw tight as she cried out in fear. The world seemed to tilt at a dangerous angle for one horrific moment before it righted once more. Sophia's heart pounded as she fought to breathe. She was all too aware that they'd almost taken a dangerous fall, but at least their pace was slowing, albeit with a choppy rhythm. And then, blessedly, they drew to a halt.

Jack swiftly dismounted and pulled Sophia down while his horse limped slightly forward while shaking its head.

"I think he might have hurt himself," Jack shouted over the howling wind. He ran a soothing hand over his horse's flank before checking its legs and hooves. "The shoe has sprung on this side. Even a gentle pace will prove a chore for him now until I have a chance to remove it."

"I can walk the rest of the way and get help," Sophia suggested. "Or maybe we could return to the Scotts' until the storm passes. I think they might be closer."

Jack glanced in each direction while shielding his eyes against the elements. "There. Is that a house?"

Sophia peered through the falling sleet

obstructing her vision and squinted when she spotted a square construction. "I've no idea."

"Come on," Jack said, and started forward. His horse limped along beside him.

"All right." Sophia didn't move. "You can seek shelter there with your horse while I go and fetch Mr. Fenmore and Edward."

"Stop it, Sophia. We're going to wait there together until this weather has passed." He jutted his chin toward the structure in the distance. "Letting you head off alone would be the height of irresponsibility on my part."

She huffed a breath, considered arguing, but decided against it when another blast of air knocked her sideways. The sleet nearly rendered her blind and while she had no wish to get stuck alone with Jack for any length of time, walking off alone in this weather would be both foolish and reckless. So she quickened her stride and hastened after his retreating form while sheets of white closed in around them. To her dismay, it looked like the storm was getting worse, not better.

"Do you know how to start a fire?" Jack asked when they stepped inside what appeared to be a shepherd's hut. Consisting of one tiny room with a stove in one corner and windows on either side, it sat on large iron wheels so it could be moved from field to field.

"I think I can manage although there are only a couple of logs in the bucket."

"Should be enough to see us through the next few hours." Jack rummaged around and eventually grabbed a fur pelt and some rope. "I'll be back in a minute."

Shaking with cold, Sophia placed one log in the stove, added a handful of kindling, and used an available tinderbox to spark a flame. By the time Jack returned, slamming the door shut behind him, a slow but steady heat was beginning to emanate from the stove. Sophia glanced at him and instantly sucked in a breath as she rushed to pull him closer to the warmth.

"What happened to your greatcoat?"

"I managed to get Star to lie down next to the hut so he keeps his weight off his foot. I've spread my great-coat and the pelt over him in an effort to keep him warm." He shrugged out of his jacket as he spoke, then went to work on his soggy cravat. His fingers were rigid, his movements jerky. "You ought to remove your wet clothes as well before the chill gets any worse."

"You…you want me to undress?" she asked. Her teeth clanked together as they chattered. She pulled her cloak tighter but all that did was make her colder as her frozen clothes pressed into her skin. "With you here?"

He gave her a look as if to say she'd be foolish to

think he might step back outside, and pulled his shirt free from his trousers. "It's up to you, but I would rather attend your wedding in three weeks from now instead of your funeral. Remember, the Scott boys didn't drown, Sophia. They perished because of the cold."

He wasn't wrong. Peter and Philip were still alive when they were pulled from the freezing water. It was the sickness that followed that killed them. With this in mind, Sophia took a step closer to the stove and stuck out her hands in an effort to warm them while doing her best to ignore the man beside her – a man who had now removed his shirt. Out of the corner of her eye she could tell he'd gone to work on his trousers. Surely he did not mean to undress completely. Did he?

The very idea that he might caused her stomach to tighten and her pulse to race. They were in a tiny space designed for one person, and Jack was in the process of getting naked. Lord help her, she had no idea what to do, where to look, much less what to say. So she kept her eyes fixed on the stove and her mouth tightly shut while telling herself to keep calm. He was just being practical. Nothing wrong with that. No sensible person could blame him for trying to stay alive, right? In fact, if she valued her own life she'd do the same.

Only she couldn't. The very idea of removing her

clothes with Jack right there was so outrageous she could not bring herself to do it.

"Sophia?"

She glanced toward him without even thinking. Big mistake.

Her breath caught in response to the hard planes of muscle that caught her eye. It was like gazing upon a perfectly sculpted work of art, only better – more impressive due to the flesh and muscle rippling with every small movement he made. Her gaze swept over his shoulders, down the length of his arms and across the firm contours defining his chest.

Before she'd looked her fill, he moved, snatching up something he promptly held toward her. "Here. Take this."

She forced her gaze to his hand and the blanket he held. The moment she grabbed it, he swung another blanket around himself, concealing his body from view.

"I strongly suggest you follow my lead," he said, his dark brown eyes meeting hers. "If it makes it any easier for you, I'll look the other way while you take off your dress."

He turned away from her. Sophia's grip on the blanket tightened. She was freezing and yet…

Swallowing, she glanced at the stove. It was doing its job but it would take forever to get her warmed up as long as she wore wet clothes. And was propriety really worth risking her health over? She considered the pros and cons. If she got undressed, no one would know besides her and Jack, and since she knew he had no interest in her in *that* way, then where was the harm? On the other hand, if she kept her clothes on, she might die.

She took a deep breath and made her decision. "I'll need your help. The closure is in the back."

There was a brief hesitation before he turned to face her. His eyes, which had been fierce with determination and concern moments earlier, were now unreadable as he said, "All right. Turn around."

She did so and felt her heart jolt when his knuckles grazed the nape of her neck.

"Are you all right?" he asked, his voice gruff as he undid the first few buttons.

"Just cold, that's all." Because there was no way on earth she would ever confess to the scorching effect he was having on her. It was electrifying, like a piece of lightning zipping along her spine.

"Don't worry. You'll heat up soon."

She almost laughed. Yes, she rather believed she would, though not because of the stove or the swift removal of her clothes, but rather because of his touch. Unable to speak, she merely nodded. And then the back of her gown was being pulled open, and she thought she heard Jack mutter a curse. But he cleared his throat and said, "I believe you can manage the rest on your own."

"Right." She glanced over her shoulder and saw that he'd turned away once more, offering her the privacy she required. "Thank you."

He made a strange sort of sound at the back of his throat. "Just tell me when you're done."

Jack's blood was on fire. And all it had taken was a tiny glimpse of Sophia's back. Most of which had been obscured by her chemise. He wrapped the rough woolen blanket tighter around himself, took a seat on a bench intended to double as a narrow bed, and removed his boots so he could peel off his trousers and smalls. It wasn't easy to do when his wet clothes clung to his skin like leeches. Or while keeping his gaze deliberately turned away from the woman undressing a few feet away.

His heart thumped in response to the one thing he'd vowed never to feel for her. Desire had always been something he'd faced with pleasure. His lovers had been experienced women who sought the same thing as he – a bit of good fun between the sheets without any further attachment after. Not to say he'd not bedded some of them numerous times. A few he'd even considered friends. But they'd always met him with open eyes and the solemn agreement that he'd never offer them more than a brief escape. And the sweet fulfillment accompanying it.

With Sophia, however, it would never be so simple. For one thing, their history would demand more from him if he made an advance. For another, she was now engaged to Edward who, while not his closest friend, was someone he respected. Third, if he took Sophia's virtue he would feel obligated to wed her, except as his father had said, she was not the sort of woman a man in his position married.

Most importantly, he was not the sort of man who got between a woman and her fiancé. He was also not the sort of man who'd be able to kiss a long-time family friend and then pretend nothing had happened.

Which left him in a bit of a bind. Because his body desperately needed, more than ever before, the one person he knew he should not want. And now he was stuck with her in a miniscule hut, naked for all the difference the blankets made since there was nothing wrong with his imagination. Just knowing she was stepping out of her clothes immediately behind him made him ache. So he sat on the bench and stared at the wall while sleet drummed down on the metal sheet roofing.

"All done," she said, her soft voice filling the air between them.

His chest tightened. He had to stay strong. For both their sakes. So he hardened his features to the best of his ability and forced his gaze toward her. Upon which he nearly growled at the unfairness of life and the manner in which fate had chosen to test him. It took every ounce of control he possessed to stay seated, to not close the distance between them and pull her into his arms, the vision she created nearly impossible to resist.

Her bonnet was gone and she'd undone her hair, the wet locks framing her beautiful face as they curled over her shoulders. Shoulders which were not only bare but smoother than silk. Then came the blanket, its stiffness concealing the curves he knew lay beneath. And finally her toes – the most perfect toes attached to the loveliest feet he'd ever seen.

Everything inside him tightened. Never in his life had he wanted to kiss a woman as much as he wanted to kiss Sophia in that moment. But he couldn't. And he wouldn't. So he fisted his hands and hardened whatever resolve he possessed, raising invisible battlements with every hope he'd survive her siege, and snatched his discarded trousers and smalls off the floor.

"Good." His voice was harder than he'd intended, but that could not be helped. He carefully stood. "Let's hang our wet clothes as best we can."

She didn't hesitate for one second. In fact, it almost seemed as though she required something with which to busy herself as much as he did. Curious that, though not an observation he'd let his mind linger on for one second. Too risky.

"While there's not much space in here for two

people," she told him in an overly bright tone, "its size allows it to heat up quickly. Which is a good thing, wouldn't you say? I mean, if we'd found a larger cottage instead, it would have taken much longer for us to warm up, don't you think?"

Jack frowned while hooking the back of his trousers onto one of several pegs attached to the wall. It sounded like she was nervous. Another thought he decided to cast from his mind. "Yes."

"In fact, I believe…" Her voice caught and he glanced at her. She was trying to hang her chemise up over one of the curtain rails, her slim arms reaching while the rest of her upper body seemed to strain against the confines of the blanket. She muttered a curse.

Jack shook himself. "Here. Let me help."

Before she had a chance to deny or accept the offer, he snatched the chemise from her hands and slipped it over the rail. There.

"Thank you. I'll…um… Perhaps there's some tea?" She spun away and proceeded to rummage through every cupboard, box, nook and cranny. Of which there were very few. She was done in less than one minute. "It doesn't look like there's much of anything."

Jack couldn't help but smile in response to her pique. She sounded exactly the same as when she'd been little and she'd set her mind on something that didn't work out. Like finding the bushes behind the mill filled with blackberries when she took him and his sisters there. Only to discover they'd been picked clean already by other children.

"It's just as well," Jack told her. "We don't have any water with which to make it. Unless we go back outside and gather some sleet, and I would personally prefer to suffer the lack of tea than have to do that. How about you?"

She turned to face him, her face all frowny and serious. "I have to agree."

He grinned. Trust Sophia to be annoyed over not being able to set her mind to something and get it done. He gestured toward the bench, the only seat available to them. "Let's get comfortable, shall we? It could be a while before we're able to leave." Especially with Star being in the condition he was now in. Jack had done his best for the horse, had managed to settle him on the sheltered side of the hut. He could only hope his greatcoat and the fur pelt would stay on and protect the mount from the elements.

Sophia glanced around as if expecting additional chairs to pop out of nowhere. Eventually she flattened her lips and traipsed to the bench with the edge of her blanket trailing behind her. Her body slid into the narrow space beside him, her shoulder grazing his.

"Sorry," she muttered, leaning away before she

pressed against him once more as she shifted. A huff of frustration left her.

Jack tried not to laugh, but couldn't quite hold back a chuckle. Their situation was by far the most unexpected and ridiculous one he'd ever found himself in. "It's fine."

She gave him an odd look. A tentative smile teased her lips. "I'm not sure any rational person would think this situation of ours is fine."

"Come now," he told her in his most cheerful tone. "This hut is undoubtedly one of the most luxurious ones of its kind. Why, the quality of the curtains alone suggests the man who bought it opted for the high end model."

The edge of her mouth twitched a few times and then her smile became a grin. "One with windows on both sides instead of only one."

"Exactly." He kept his gaze on her, his chest filling with warmth on account of the sparkle he saw in her eyes. He'd caused that, he reflected with pride, by turning a somewhat disastrous situation into a humorous one. He leaned his shoulder against the wall and turned a little in order to better face her, the movement pushing his knee into hers. To his satisfaction, she did not shy away as she'd done when her shoulder bumped his, and he relaxed into his new position. He liked that point of shared contact. It pulled him back through time to when he and Sophia had been like…

Finding the right word was a struggle. They'd never been like brother and sister, but they'd always been closer than friends, the connection they'd built through their shared sense of humor and interests, a bond unlike any other. That was before his father had opened his eyes to the woman Sophia was growing into and to all the restrictions he suddenly ought to consider. Because he was the heir to an earl, and she nothing more than a foundling two upstanding people had taken pity on.

He flinched at the harsh reality as it swept over his shoulders. And then again when he allowed himself to face the truth he'd been running from these past four years. If Sophia had been the daughter of a respectable couple, if her parents had been gentry, then he would have started courting her as soon as he'd become aware of her as a woman.

Because he knew without doubt they'd get along. With her, he would be happy, and he rather believed she would be happy with him as well. But there was something more – deeper emotions linking his heart with hers. He felt it at the core of his being. Had always done so. But since the emotion would likely make him miserable if it began to take root, he tamped it down as he always did before it had a chance to destroy him.

After all, he could not have her. She'd always been destined to marry another. Edward, as it turned out.

Jack's gut twisted with displeasure. He forced that feeling aside as well and made himself think of something else. Like the fact that he had been given a chance to re-connect with Sophia. It was an opportunity he ought not to waste. And so he said, "Remember how we used to hunt for bird's nests in the spring?"

"We'd get a point for each one we found and the winner would then receive a medal." She gave him a look. "Do you still have it?"

"The medal?" It had been made from the lid of a discarded tin. Jack and Edward had helped each other flatten the edges by hammering it with a rock. A knife had been used to create a small slit so the ribbon Sophia donated could be slipped through it and tied. He nodded. "It should be at Eastgate in a box under my bed."

"Your sisters would usually tire of the game, but I always loved it. Even now, I'm drawn to the chirping of chicks."

"How many nests did you find last spring?"

"I've no idea," she said, affording him a look that suggested the contrary.

He grinned and pushed her knee with his own. "Liar."

She smiled at him broadly, until he wished he could freeze that moment in time forever and keep it in his pocket. "Very well. I found six."

"Only six?" He feigned a look of shock. "Why

Sophia, I fear your nest finding skills have failed you."

A playful swat landed on his arm. "I don't have time for that sort of thing anymore. I'm busier now."

"With the church and its parishioners?"

"There's so much to do and I'm happy to help. It fills me with a wonderful sense of purpose."

"I'm pleased to hear it." He hesitated a second before he asked, "Do you think you'll continue this work once you're Edward's wife?"

"I don't see why not. He's already helping with some of his father's sermons, cementing his position. Once he gets his own parish, my work will likely increase rather than diminish."

Jack frowned as he met her gaze. He couldn't help it any more than he could the next words he spoke. "I just don't see you being a vicar's wife, Sophia."

She started as if he'd jabbed her. "Why on earth not?"

"It's too grave a position for someone as flighty as you."

"Flighty?"

"No... I mean... That's not the right word." He sighed in frustration. "Forgive me, it's just that this serious role you've crafted for yourself doesn't match your lively and spontaneous spirit. As a child—"

"I've not been a child for some years now, Jack. People grow up and as they do, they change."

"To some degree, I'll grant you, but they don't become completely different people and—"

"There's nothing wrong with wanting to help those in need. I'll not allow you to fault me for finding comfort in the work I'm doing."

"Of course not. I didn't mean to imply that I did. It's just…you were never able to sit still for any great length of time. Whenever I'd see you during Sunday service your gaze would be wandering everywhere, and as soon as the service was done, you'd usually hurry outside as if desperate to flee. Because you hated being forced indoors for any duration of time and because…" A memory, piercingly sharp, caught hold of his mind.

"What?" she asked, her brow wrinkling slightly.

"You always insisted God couldn't be found in a building – that if one wished to find Him, one had to go out into nature."

"I remember," she said, her voice but a whisper.

"And yet you intend to bind yourself to a man who will force you into the very church you wish to escape, every day of the week. A man with whom you disagree on something elementally defining. Edward is going to be a vicar, Sophia, a man for whom the church encompasses God's very essence."

Her jaw tightened. She gave her head a swift shake. "What are you doing, Jack?"

"I don't know what you mean."

"Edward and I have known each other for what feels like forever. We understand each other, even if there are matters on which our opinions differ. He is willing to give me the protection of his good name, which is more than any other man has ever offered me or is likely to offer me in the future. To say no to him would be incredibly foolish on my part, even if I do have to spend every day indoors, listening to scripture that doesn't make me feel the least bit closer to God. But what does help – what does distract me from the gnawing ache of knowing I'll never be able to marry the man I…" She sucked in a breath and stood, eyes wide with horror. Backing away, she shook her head. "It doesn't matter. As long as I'm able to do some good, then that's enough. It has to be enough."

He stared at her while his heart pounded hard against his chest. Hope gripped his stomach, turning it upside down while heat washed over his skin. He got up as well and stalked toward her, only stopping when she raised her hand.

"The man you what, Sophia?" His voice was hoarse, his body vibrating with the need to discover the truth.

She stared at him for a long drawn-out moment before she finally shook her head once more and said, "Nothing."

Disappointment gripped his muscles, instilling in

him a dangerous mixture of anger and pain. She was lying to him and the realization of this caused him to act. His hands came up of their own volition and gripped her arms hard. She gasped, but he didn't let go. "Tell me, Sophia."

"Stop it, Jack."

"Not until you tell me who you'd rather marry instead."

"I can't!"

"Why?"

"Because it would make no difference," she said as tears clogged her throat. "Because the confession would only make everything worse."

He searched her eyes and found so much pain there it stabbed at his chest. "You're certain of this?"

She stared back at him. "I don't know why we're discussing this, Jack. It's a pointless issue."

"What about this, Sophia?" He knew he was being rash and that she might hate him for what he was driven to do. But he couldn't seem to stop himself any longer. So he drew her closer and dipped his head. "Is this a pointless issue too?"

6

CHAPTER SIX

Sophia knew she shouldn't allow him to kiss her – was keenly aware her heart would likely break in the aftermath. But in this moment, this brief illusion Jack offered, she had no choice but to give in to his advance. It was, after all, like a dream come true – his mouth on hers, an exchange of breath, and the feel of his hand pressing into her back as he held her close.

She sighed against the touch of his lips, firm yet soft as they swept over hers in sweet exploration. Her fingers stole over his shoulders, tracing the muscle there as they crept higher, giving herself the freedom to touch him as she'd yearned to do for so long. Her hands found each other, forming a loop around his neck. His teeth scraped her flesh, nibbling gently, inquiring if she desired more without attempting to force the issue.

Alive with the wonder of this shared closeness and how right it felt, she parted her lips and granted him entry while arching into his solid frame. He made a rough sound – a rumbling of sorts – and guided her backward.

"Sophia." Her name was but a guttural sound, nearly lost in the kiss.

But she heard it, the raw emotion in his voice provoking feelings she'd tried so hard to bury. And as he lowered himself to the bench and pulled her into his lap, she clung to him with all she was, desperate to imprint this moment upon her brain – all too aware that it could not last.

Later, after this stolen haven in time, she'd have to face reality. A world in which she and Jack would never be able to have each other. She'd have to face Edward. His name fluttered through her mind even as she spoke Jack's. He wrapped his arms tighter around her, encouraging her to sink against him. His fingers were in her damp hair while he drank from her as if parched. The blanket he wore had slipped to his waist, allowing her to press her palm to his chest.

Hot skin stretching across firm planes of muscle greeted her touch. All traces of the chill creeping over the winter landscape outside had been completely erased. It made it so easy for her to forget.

And yet, Edward's name persisted, forcing her to withdraw on an intake of breath. She bent her head against Jack's shoulder and fought for the strength she required to walk away. "We need to end this."

Right now. Before they did something that could not be undone. She was keenly aware of her state of undress, aware that one swift tug would undo the blanket protecting her modesty, and equally aware that she was one second away from throwing all caution to the wind and letting Jack take her. If he wished to.

"I am engaged to Edward," she murmured while Jack smoothed a hand over her head. "I'll not dishonor him by lying with you."

"Tell me something, Sophia." He spoke quietly, the words falling slowly from his mouth. "Do you love me?"

His question would have caused her to leap from him had he not held her firmly in place. "That's a terrible thing to ask."

"Do you?"

"Jack…"

"Look at me, Sophia." When she failed to respond, he placed his fingers beneath her chin and nudged it upward. Stormy eyes, dark with intensity, held her captive. "Tell me you love me and I swear I'll find a way for us to be together."

"How?"

"I… I don't know yet."

Not reassuring by any means. Nor was it the sort of declaration she'd need in order to walk away from the security Edward offered. She shook her head and pulled away from Jack's touch. "I'm sorry."

"Sophia, you cannot kiss me as you just did and then deny there's a deep connection between us." His hand settled on her shoulder, pinning her before she could add more distance. "Would it help if I were to confess my own love for you?"

"What?" She turned, the bliss she'd recently found in his arms replaced by a sudden anger brought on by confusion.

"I love you, Sophia. I realize now that I've done so for years." He raised his hand as if he intended to caress her cheek.

She swatted it away and gave him a hard look. "Then why did you ignore my letters? Why did you stay away for so long? You gave me no reason to hope, no reason to think you even cared. Rather, I was granted the opposite with every awful piece of gossip I read about you."

"I'm sorry if I hurt you. Doing so was never my intention, but marrying you was impossible and—"

"That's the heart of it. Isn't it, Jack? I'm an unsuitable match for most men, but especially for a peer. So why would you tell me you love me now? What on earth am I supposed to do with that knowledge other than suffer more because of it?"

His eyes widened just enough to convey surprise. He clearly did not understand her position, and proceeded to say as much. "I thought you'd be pleased to know I return your affection."

"Pleased? How can I be pleased when it doesn't change anything for the better? Unless you have suddenly chosen to make me your wife and have found a way to do so in a manner that will not humiliate Edward or his parents in the process." When he said nothing, she huffed a breath and turned away, tears stinging her eyes. "Then your declaration makes no difference. At least before you said anything, I could accept the decision I made to marry Edward, but now…"

Jack stepped closer and wound his arms around her, offering strength even as she railed at him. "I'm sorry. I wish I had said something sooner so you could have had the option of being my—"

The abruptness with which he cut himself off made her blink. She swiped her watery eyes with her hand and turned in his arms. Tilting her head back, she gazed up at him, hoping he'd not been about to suggest what she thought. "Of being your what?"

He dipped his head and kissed her. "Nothing, Sophia. It's too late for that now anyway. I'm sorry."

She placed her palm against his chest and shoved. "I could have been your what, Jack? Your wife? Because I think we can both agree you would not have proposed, so what were you thinking just now? That I could have lowered myself to be your mistress? Is that it?"

Discomfort seeped into his eyes, giving him a lost sort of look that tore at her heart. She forced herself to stay strong, to put up barriers one by one so she wouldn't crumble.

"I would have taken care of you," he whispered.

She stared at him, at the man she loved so desperately she'd have dived into a frozen lake in order to save him, offered her life for his. Only it wasn't enough. It never had been. "You didn't even have the courage to tell me how you feel until it was too late."

"I didn't realize how I feel, how I have always felt, until now." He raked his fingers through his hair. Frustration lent a wild expression to his eyes. "I'm sorry, Sophia. For everything."

"Me too." What a mess. When she'd risen that morning she'd been satisfied with her decision to marry Edward. Now, she looked forward to a future filled with more regret and heartache than she could bear.

All because Jack claimed he loved her. Because if he really did, then it was worse knowing they were prevented from being together because she wasn't good enough for him. Accepting that he didn't want her would have been easier. She would have made peace with that. Now, she feared she would always live with regret.

She crossed to the window and looked out over the dreary landscape. "It looks like the sleet is letting up. I probably ought to get back to the vicarage."

"Your clothes won't be dry yet."

"No, but they won't get any wetter at this point either, and the last thing I'd want is for Edward to come looking for me and find me here like this with you. He doesn't deserve that."

"I know."

Jack's words settled heavily on her shoulders. He would not thwart the rules of Society for her, would not stand up to his parents and tell them he would marry her no matter what. It was what she ought to expect, yet it still crushed her heart and numbed her soul. "I'll get dressed then and be on my way."

Jack wanted to howl at the injustice of it all. He wanted to drive his fist into something hard until his knuckles bled. Because focusing on that pain would be so much easier than dealing with the shredded remains of his heart.

She was gone.

Without a trace.

He glanced around at the shed's sparse interior where his clothes still hung to dry. It was almost as if she'd never been there at all – as if their glorious kiss had never happened. Only the fire still burning in the stove served as proof of her recent presence. She'd lit that while he'd seen to Star.

Lord help him, he was an idiot of the worst kind. Instead of correcting the misplaced assumption she'd made about him saying mistress rather than wife, he'd let her think the worst.

Why?

Why hadn't he told her of his father's threat or that he'd worked to release himself from it? Why hadn't he let her know that he was now free to marry the woman of his own choosing?

Because of Edward and because it was simpler. Because breaking off an engagement had consequences. To promise her the moon and the stars when he'd no idea if he could provide them would be unfair. Better then to let her hate him a little longer while he tried to figure things out.

Feeling drained, he forced himself into action. Star would need to be cared for and Jack himself would require a large glass of brandy after what he'd just been through. So he grabbed his still-damp shirt and flung it over his head. A shudder raked through him as cold linen met his warm skin. He moved closer to the stove and put the rest of his clothes on there, then snuffed the flames, removing all lingering evidence of this afternoon's secret encounter.

"What on earth happened to you?" Felicity asked when he traipsed through the foyer more than one hour later after making sure Star would be cared for by competent stable hands. His boots squelched with every step he took. "Did you fall into the river?"

"No," Jack grumbled. He walked straight past her and started up the stairs.

"I trust you'll dry off and return downstairs so you can help entertain our guests?"

"They're here to see you, not me," he told her over his shoulder without breaking his stride. Reaching the landing, he took a sharp turn, reached his bedchamber, and disappeared inside. All he wanted right now was to be alone.

Of course, that was impossible with a house full of guests. Especially since the reason he'd returned to Eastgate in the first place was to help entertain them. As he discovered, playing cards and billiards with them actually helped. They were all good sports, entertaining him and his sisters with stories, quelling the ache in his chest enough for him to feel somewhat normal.

"There's something I need to ask you," he told Felicity the next day while Kaitlin went for a stroll in the garden with Madsen and Irving. The rest of the gentlemen who'd risen later still sat over breakfast, allowing Jack a rare opportunity to catch his sister alone.

"Yes?" Felicity angled her head with interest. They were in the music room where she'd been practicing one of her favorite pieces as she often did in the mornings.

Jack sat beside her on the bench in front of the piano. "Are you at all interested in any of these men courting you?"

Her lips parted. She blinked a few times. "What a strange question."

"I simply wonder if there might be someone else, another man who may have caught your interest. Because if there is, I'd hate to see you settle for someone you do not care for."

Felicity held his gaze a moment, then dipped her chin and gave her attention to the keys. She traced a few of them with her fingers. "Why would you suppose there's anyone else?"

Unwilling to reveal Sophia's suggestion there might be, he said, "You just don't seem as interested in our guests as I thought you would be. Right now, three of them are in the dining room and yet you are here. Alone."

"You know I always play in the morning."

"I do."

"And I am a person of habit, Jack."

"Agreed."

When he said nothing further, she eventually told him, "We cannot always have what we want. Can we?"

The hopelessness with which she spoke nearly broke him. It was the same kind of despondent sadness he felt, reflected back at him by one of the people he loved most of all. "Felicity?"

She tried a smile, but it wobbled before disappearing completely. "He and I are all wrong for each other. We always have been, and wishing things were different isn't going to solve anything. My only recourse is to move on, bury these foolish feelings, and try to be happy with what I have. Which is, in fact, quite a lot when compared with so many others. I've no right to complain."

Nor did he, he supposed. And yet he could not stop himself from feeling as though he was being denied the quintessence of what made life worth living. All because he was privileged. He scoffed and shook his head. What utter tripe.

"What is it?" Felicity asked.

"Nothing," he said since the alternative would involve him unburdening himself, and that wasn't something he was ready to do that morning. But maybe she would confide in him? "If there's anything I can do to help you win the hand of the man who—"

"Thank you, Jack, but there isn't, and speaking of it will not make that fact any easier."

"I'm sorry." Was it just him, or was that becoming the most popular phrase of late?

She offered a smile, turned a page of sheet music, and started on a lively tune.

Jack sat for a moment and watched her play

before he stood and went to help Mr. Richmond complete the repairs on his roof as promised. Later, he'd inquire if any of the gentlemen might want to help him fetch a Yule log from the woods. That ought to keep him busy for a few extra hours. Afterward, he'd have to think of something else to take his mind off Sophia, from Felicity's heartbreaking revelation so similar to his own, and from the weight bearing down on his soul.

Little did he know that things were about to get worse. His parents would not allow him to stay home from church on Sunday. Not when all the guests wished to go and certainly not when he'd always been known to accompany his family to the weekly service. Even when they'd been in London.

So here he was now, gritting his teeth while Mr. Fenmore called the banns for Sophia and Edward. It was horrific. Like a carriage crash he could not look away from. Doing so was made all the harder due to his family's status, which reserved them seats at the front of the church. As it happened, the spot made available to him today was located immediately behind the vicar's son and his bride-to-be.

Jack stared at the back of Sophia's neck, at the way in which her dove-gray bonnet curved along her hairline. Her pelisse collar started one inch lower, but in between, there was a tantalizing display of bare skin. His fingers twitched with the fierce desire to reach up and stroke his way across it. For now that he'd kissed her, held her in his arms and knew how smooth she was to the touch, he was tempted by her more than ever before.

"Jack."

Kaitlin's voice, a low whisper, dragged his gaze from the source of his interest. "Yes?"

"Are you all right?"

Not by a long shot. "Yes."

She frowned at him. "Then why do you look like you're about to murder someone?"

He scowled at her. "I'm fine."

Only he wasn't. His insides were twisted so tightly he could scarcely breathe, his posture so rigid he feared he might snap at any moment. So when the service drew to an end and he had the chance to escape, he took it. Without one word to his parents or siblings or the guests whose company he was meant to keep, Jack left the church and made for the nearest inn.

Which was where Edward found him ten minutes later.

"What's with you?" he asked once he'd dropped into the chair opposite Jack's. He gestured for a serving maid to bring another pint of beer. "You're not really known for your foul moods so why the nasty glower?"

Jack flattened his mouth and did his best to ease the tension putting his body on edge. "It's just a short spell of irritation. Nothing that won't sort itself out in time." He took a sip of his beer and savored the freshness. Edward's tankard arrived and he too took a swig.

"You've also never been much of a liar." Edward folded his arms on the table and leaned forward. "If I were to guess, I'd say you're starting to realize you want something that won't be as easy for you to win as a game of cards or a curricle race."

"Leave it be, Edward. I don't want to talk about it."

"I just might have to insist when it concerns me directly." He raised an eyebrow. "I'm not blind, Jack, and I've known you long enough to have a sense of how your mind works."

Jack snorted in attempt to hide his rising dread. "I doubt that."

"All right. Let's put my belief to the test, shall we?" When Jack shrugged, Edward said, "Growing up, you and Sophia were always thick as thieves. She may have been five years younger than us, but her interests always seemed to align with yours. I was the sensible one – the bore, if you will – who always chose to sit quietly with Felicity and Kaitlin while you and Sophia chased each other all over creation. As time went by, Sophia got older. She grew up and transformed, and as she did so, you started seeing her in a new light."

"I've no idea what you're talking about."

"No?" Edward gave him a, don't-take-me-for-a-fool sort of look. "I saw your expression when I escorted her to her first assembly hall dance four years ago. Your eyes lit up, amazement took over, and for the rest of the evening you could not tear your gaze away from her. You danced two sets and then, the very next day, you were gone, as if something had frightened the hell out of you. Perhaps the realization that you were in love with someone you didn't think you could marry?"

"She was but eighteen years of age," Jack snapped as the final thread of his frayed control slipped between his fingers. "It would have been wrong to pursue her. It still is, damn it. She's meant to marry you!"

Edward stared at him with unnerving steadiness. "The only reason I proposed is because you refused to fight for her. If you wish to do so, however, I will step aside."

Jack caught himself holding his breath and slowly expelled it. "It's too late for that, isn't it?"

"It will be once we're married."

Dropping his gaze to his tankard, Jack stared into the amber liquid while trying to put his thoughts in order. Four years ago he'd been three and twenty years of age. He'd only just inherited his honorary title after his grandfather's passing, when his father had become the Earl of Turner. And he'd been painfully aware of the duty his new position demanded. Having his father tell him outright that

Sophia would not be an option for him when it came to seeking a wife had been intolerable. Jack had been furious with his father, not because he'd suggested Jack might consider marrying Sophia, but because of the threat.

Or so he'd convinced himself.

In truth, being denied Sophia had been the real heart of the matter, one he'd refused to face. But looking back, it was hard not to when the women he'd bedded in the time since had all had dark blonde hair, just like Sophia. While he'd excused the affairs by telling himself he'd offered each one of these women comfort, the truth was he'd sought it, a means by which to pretend if even for the briefest of moments Sophia was his.

He curled his hand into a tight fist and swore beneath his breath while every belief he'd forced upon himself in recent years began to crumble. His love for Sophia was real and powerful, and no amount of running away would make it vanish.

"I only have two choices." He raised his gaze to Edward's.

"Yes?"

"I can either resign myself to a miserable life without her, or I can fight for the future I think we both want. Neither will be easy, but there's no doubt in my mind as to which road will lead to the greatest reward. If I'm successful."

"So then?"

"My father will oppose the idea, but it's not as if I really need his approval." Now that he had amassed his own fortune, he didn't need his allowance or the inheritance. "If Sophia and I…" Jack blinked as a crazy idea took root in his brain. He was reaching for straws out of sheer desperation – he knew this – and yet he could not help but ask, "If I were to procure a special license, would you then be able to marry us? I know it's a great favor to ask, all things considered, but it would allow us to wed before Papa has a chance to react."

Edward smiled, his mouth stretching wide in a way Jack had never seen before. "I would be honored to officiate."

"No hard feelings?"

"None whatsoever, provided you don't muck this up, and you take care to treat her well."

Jack's heart began thumping with renewed excitement. "You have my word, Edward. I'll do my best on both counts."

CHAPTER SEVEN

BRIGHT GREEN PINE garlands tied with red ribbons were strung above windows and doorways when Sophia arrived at the assembly hall Christmas dance several days later, accompanied by Edward and his parents. She'd not spoken to Jack since leaving him at the shepherd's hut and had even asked Edward to deliver the lemons and honey she'd promised Mrs. Richmond so she wouldn't run into him when he went to work on the roof.

As it turned out, this had been the right decision. According to Edward, Jack had already been at the Richmond house when he arrived with her delivery. Later, when Kaitlin and Felicity invited Sophia for tea at their home, Sophie turned them down. Going to Eastgate Abbey right now was much too risky, so she used excessive wedding preparations as an excuse.

But in spite of the effort she made to avoid Jack, Sophia was not able to do so forever. She had been keenly aware of his presence in church this past Sunday. It was as if his eyes had burned a hole in the nape of her neck during the service, warming her skin and flushing her cheeks.

The memory of the kiss they'd shared lingered, like a spot of stubborn paint upon her lips. Worse was what it had led to, not just the angst or confusion, the wish to flee from all she knew and simply disappear, but the dreams of them being together. Each night when she prepared for bed, she prayed she'd find herself swept away in his arms, even as she hoped she wouldn't. The contradiction of what she wanted and did not want was driving her mad, each heated kiss and intimate touch she shared with him while asleep, more so.

And as a result, guilt constantly gnawed at her conscience, for it was Edward she was going to marry. Not Jack.

"I see they've forgotten the mistletoe," Edward said as he led her into the dance hall. An aromatic scent of cooked meats wafted toward them from the supper room on the right – a reminder that there was food to be had, should they get hungry.

"They probably don't want to risk someone taking advantage," Sophia said while instinctively searching for the one man she both longed to see and escape from in equal measure.

"It looks like a new set is beginning," Edward said while leading her into the crowded space. "Shall we dance?"

"Would it not be best for us to wait for your parents?" Sophia glanced over her shoulder at where the Fenmores stood. They appeared to have been waylaid by some friends.

"I can think of no reason to do so. Come, Sophia, we are to be married after all."

The reminder made her heart hurt all over again. But since she loved Edward and none of this mess was his fault, she did her best to smile for his sake. He did have a point after all. They were to be married and it would be wrong of her to ruin what ought to be a happy occasion by being glum.

So she pressed herself closer to him and allowed him to lead her toward the dance floor. They took their positions opposite each other in preparation for the country dance about to commence, and when the lively tune began, she met him halfway. They spun and skipped while weaving a path between other dancers until Sophia was laughing with joy. She caught Edward's gaze, which was always so somber, and found herself slightly entranced by the unexpected sparkle within it. A grin swiftly followed and her own smile broadened as they danced their way back in line. Whatever her feelings for Jack, she and Edward would find a shared rhythm.

Sophia took comfort in that.

"Would you care for refreshment?" Edward asked once the set had concluded and they'd moved toward the periphery of the room. "I am personally out of breath and parched."

"A glass of lemonade would be welcome," Sophia said. "If such is available."

"I'm sure it is." He steered her along, halting now and then to offer greetings to friends.

"There you are!" Felicity's familiar voice prompted Sophia and Edward to turn as one.

"We just arrived five minutes ago," Kaitlin said as she sidled up next to her sister. "What a crush."

Behind them stood Jack, handsome as ever in his evening attire. His dark eyes seemed to pin Sophia in place. "Miss Fenmore. It's a pleasure to see you again. You too, Mr. Fenmore."

Heat filled Sophia's cheeks before bathing her completely. Captivated by the intensity of Jack's stare, she gazed at him while blood rushed through her veins. She forced herself to acknowledge his sisters and smile as if all was as it should be – as if she and Jack had not recently worn nothing but blankets while sharing a scandalous kiss.

"I'm so pleased to see all of you again," she said. "We scarcely had a chance to chat after Sunday service." Sophia had gotten caught up in conversation with Mrs. Scott immediately after the service. When the lady had finished thanking her for the wonderful contents of the basket Sophia delivered,

Felicity, Kaitlin, Jack, and Edward had all been gone.

"We are rather busy these days with our gentlemen suitors," Kaitlin explained. "In fact, I'm afraid you must excuse me since I promised Lord Cumberland the next dance."

"I would be honored if you would partner with me for it," Jack told Sophia once Kaitlin had left.

Fearful of how she might respond to even his most innocent touch, Sophia moved closer to Edward. "I'm not sure…um…that is to say, I—"

"Go on, Sophia. Dance with Jack." Edward collected two glasses of lemonade from a passing server and handed one to Sophia, the other to Felicity. "I'll dance with Miss Lancaster in the meantime."

Sophia frowned as she sipped her drink. Was she imagining things, or did Felicity look as though she were about to be tortured? Her expression – the hope and yearning mixed with painful resignation – was so familiar it took Sophia no more than a second to place it. And when she did, she nearly gasped, then promptly drank some more lemonade to hide her reaction.

Dear Lord. Was it possible the man her friend pined for was Edward? If so, was Edward aware? And if so, did he return Felicity's affection?

The chance he did but that he might not think he was fit to court an earl's daughter pierced Sophia's heart with such shattering force she almost winced.

She glanced at him – at the man who'd been like a brother to her for most of her life – and noted the hint of sadness about his eyes.

"Miss Fenmore?"

Jack's voice, firm and sure, pulled her out of her reverie. She set her glass aside and accepted the arm he offered. Before he could lead her off, she told Felicity and Edward, "Enjoy your dance."

Edward's lips parted as if he meant to respond, but then the moment passed, and Sophia was whisked away by Jack while Edward gave his attention to the woman Sophie believed he truly loved. Heavens, what a tangle.

"I've missed you," Jack murmured close to her ear. He'd guided her to the spot where she was meant to stand in preparation for the next country dance. His hand slid discreetly along her arm, his fingertips grazing her waist right before he withdrew them. "And I've every intention of making you mine. Don't marry Edward."

He'd stepped away before she could register what he had said, leaving her body reeling in the wake of his touch. The implication of his words, spoken in this crowded place where anyone might overhear, was more than scandalous. It was ruinous.

She narrowed her gaze on him. He merely smirked, his eyes burning bright with devilish mischief. It wasn't until the dance was underway and she stepped toward him that she had a chance to respond. "You can't be serious."

He held her gaze while he wrapped one arm around her waist, turning her about in time to the music. There was nothing abnormal in his movements. He followed the steps with faultless fluidity. And yet the heat from his hand burned through her dress to warm her back, the press of his palm more insistent than what was proper, yet too unobtrusive for anyone else to notice.

One of his black eyebrows rose in challenge. "I've never been more so."

She wanted to argue, to shout at him for being unfair. He could not do this to her. Not now after she'd spent years adjusting to the idea of having to marry another, to the painful reality of Jack not wanting her, and to the fact that even if he did she'd never be good enough for him. But the dance prevented her from saying any of this as she was forced to take a few turns with other gentlemen.

Sophia did her best to smile and to look as though she enjoyed herself even though she'd never been more on edge in her life. It felt like an avalanche barreled toward her, and she stood no chance of outrunning it.

The gentleman with whom she'd been dancing released her to another, prompting her to blink as she gazed up into Edward's familiar eyes. His lips quirked. "You look extremely put out, Sophia. Is Jack provoking you?"

"Yes. I mean, no. I mean…" She wasn't sure of anything anymore. Her thoughts were in chaos.

Edward guided her between two other couples. "He cares for you. More than you know."

Her heart started pounding. She needed to know where he stood in all of this. The last thing she wanted to do was hurt him. "As you care for Felicity?"

His eyes dimmed. A swift nod was all it took for him to confide his deepest secret before he spun her back toward Jack.

"We need to speak."

"Yes," she agreed. She wasn't sure what was happening tonight but she felt like her life was about to change. Whether or not for the better, she couldn't be certain. But she had her own concerns to air. For although she did not believe she and Jack stood a chance of being together, how could she speak her vows to Edward when he and she both loved other people? To do so would be wrong. And when it came to Edward and Felicity, Sophia believed Jack to be the only person who might be able to help.

"This way," Jack said once the dance had ended. He'd caught her by her arm and was guiding her toward a door at the opposite end of the room. He tried the handle and, finding it unlocked, ushered her into the dimly lit salon beyond.

"We can't be in here alone." Sophie pulled away from him and turned. "What if someone saw us sneaking away together?"

"No one did. I checked." He crossed his arms and studied her. "Now come here, Sophia, so I may kiss you."

"Jack, I…"

"Yes?"

Confusion and want collided. "What are you doing?"

"Being as forthright as I know how." He unfolded his arms and moved toward her. "You and I have spent years hiding our feelings, playing pretend, and hoping things would sort themselves out in the end. But they won't. Not unless we can be honest with each other, which I'll admit may require some courage."

She searched his eyes, the depth of emotion she found there so intense she caught her breath. "What are you saying, Jack?"

He raised one hand and cupped her cheek, the soft abrasiveness of his thumb sliding over her skin to produce a surge of warmth deep within. "I love you, Sophia. I've done so for years, but my father…" His jaw tightened and she saw him flex his fingers. When he spoke next, his voice was strained. "I left because of him, added distance and tried to force us both to stop dreaming of something impossible so we could face reality instead. It was stupid. Of course it didn't work. And then I learned you were marrying Edward."

"Only because I knew I could never have you." Her eyes stung in response to his words. She felt a tear slide between her lashes. He brushed it aside with his thumb, then leaned in and kissed her. Not with overwhelming passion this time, but tenderly, as though he sought to give her comfort.

"I'm sorry for the pain I've caused you." He leaned his forehead against hers and pulled her into his arms.

"You told me you wished I wouldn't get married because at least then I could be your mistress."

He took a deep breath. Released it. "I never said any such thing. You made the assumption that I would have said mistress rather than wife. My mistake was failing to correct you."

"Why didn't you?"

"Because the situation was complicated. I didn't want to give you false hope. But that has since changed. I've spoken with Edward and know now what I must do."

"And what's that, Jack?"

"Risk it all – everything – for the one thing that matters." He leaned back and focused his gaze on her with forceful resolve. "My father won't approve and neither will Society, but they can all go hang as far as

I am concerned, because this is my life, my future, and I mean to spend every waking moment of it with you. If you'll have me, that is. Marry me, Sophia, be my wife, and let me love you with all that I am."

"But I…I mean… How would we manage to do so?" She blinked. "You said you spoke with Edward?"

"I did and he has given his blessing. He'll even marry us in secret if that is what we wish. My thought was to procure a special license and get the deed done before anyone has a chance to protest."

"That's not a good plan." She worried her lip. "Edward will be ridiculed if his fiancée marries another. Especially now that the first set of banns have been called. So will his parents, and after all they have done for me, I cannot treat them so thoughtlessly."

"Officially breaking off the engagement will likely have a similar effect," Jack said.

"Unless it became known that Edward's heart was engaged elsewhere. If he were to form another attachment, then you and I would be free to marry immediately after without being criticized for it, I should think. Most people love a good romance. They also appreciate a good story of thwarting adversity. So they might be inclined to forgive and forget how the happily ever afters came about. Provided we play this right."

Jack frowned. "Are you saying Edward would rather marry someone else?"

"Yes."

"But who?"

She steeled herself for his reaction. "Your sister. Felicity."

His mouth dropped open. Shock widened his eyes. And then, as if she'd just handed him the missing piece to a complicated puzzle, he said, "He never suggested any such thing. I wonder why?"

"Isn't it obvious? Edward doesn't think he stands a chance. Felicity is an earl's daughter and he's just a vicar's son."

"He's gentry, though, and the Fenmores are respectable people. My parents have always spoken highly of them."

"But would they approve a match between Felicity and Edward?"

Jack firmed his lips. "I'll do my best to ensure it, though doing so may be easier if he's no longer attached to you. Sophia, you're absolutely right to formally break things off with him. It must be done. For everyone's sake."

"And if I do, you'll marry me?"

"In a heartbeat." He hugged her tightly before seeking her mouth with his own. His hands drew her flush against him, molding her to his more solid frame. Unlike the previous kiss, this one was fierce, hungry, and full of promise.

"You won't mind facing your parents' condemnation?" she whispered while pressing her cheek to his chest moments later. "I fear they'll be angry with you for throwing your future away on me."

His hold tightened and she felt his chest vibrate in response to a growl. "Like I said, I don't care if they disapprove. You're the woman I want – the woman I choose – and nothing is going to stand in my way of winning you any longer."

Comforted by his fortitude and slightly awed by it too, Sophia leaned back and smiled at him with all the love she held in her heart. "Then I must speak with Edward."

CHAPTER EIGHT

WHILE SOPHIA WORKED on undoing her attachment to Edward during the following days, Jack decided to have a heart-to-heart conversation with Felicity. However, it had been nearly impossible for him to seek her out in private since the assembly hall dance, during which it appeared she'd attracted Viscount Cumberland's and Mr. Irving's interests. The two men had practically been glued to her ever since.

So Jack eventually decided to knock on her bedchamber door one afternoon while everyone else enjoyed an afternoon nap. It took a moment before she admitted him, her expression one of surprise when she saw who had come to call. "How out of the ordinary, Jack. I rather expected Kaitlin, Mama, or one of the maids."

"I hope I'm not disturbing your rest?"

"Not too much. I was working on a drawing if you must know."

"I see." He glanced beyond her shoulder and spotted her sketchpad on the bed. Returning his gaze to hers he asked, "May I come in?"

"Of course." She moved aside and he stepped past her. The door closed with a soft click. Once he knew no one else would overhear, he turned toward his sister and said, "I've asked Sophia to marry me."

"What?"

"Perhaps you're not aware, but the fact is, I've loved her since forever, and when I learned I might lose her I—"

A squeal of delight cut him off and then Felicity's arms were around him, squeezing him with all her might. Good grief. He coughed and sputtered, prompting her to release him.

"Sorry, Jack. I'm just so incredibly pleased."

"I thought you might be." He met her gaze evenly. "Especially since this means Edward won't be getting married either."

Felicity sucked in a breath and spun toward the window. Her fingertips pressed into the pane of glass as she stared out across the barren winter land-scape. "What are you implying?"

"I think you know."

She swallowed, appeared to straighten herself, and finally faced him. "He doesn't feel the same way about me or he would have said something. At the very least, he would not have asked Sophia to be his wife."

Her eyes, which had grown watery as she spoke, spilled over. She sniffed and averted her gaze once more, clearly embarrassed by her lack of composure.

Jack pulled a handkerchief from his pocket and handed it to her. "There's a good chance he's as big an idiot as I am."

"Pardon?" She dabbed her eyes and blew her nose.

"I didn't tell Sophia how I felt either, mostly because I tried to ignore the yearnings of my heart. Instead, I made some drastic decisions which could have had serious consequences on all of our lives."

"You should have fought for her when you realized you loved her. I'm sure Papa and Mama would have given their blessing. After all, they've welcomed Sophia into our home since that one time when Kaitlin and I invited her over to see our kittens. We met during Sunday tea at the vicarage after church, if you will recall. I don't think Kaitlin and I were older than four."

"I remember it well." Seating had been limited so his sisters had sat in his lap. Until they'd scampered off and hidden beneath the table with Sophia. No one had minded. In fact, the adults had all pretended there was nothing amiss. "However, this realization of mine has been rather recent. Struck me like a punch to the face if you must know. And Papa will not give his blessing. Right before I left he said…"

Felicity tilted her head in question. "What?"

"Nothing." Repeating the insult his father had dealt Sophia would only make him angry once more. "The point is I've only one option if I am to make Sophia my wife, and that is to wed her in secret."

Felicity's hands flew to her mouth. "No, Jack. You can't do that."

"Once it is done, however, I fear Papa will refuse to listen to reason, so if you wish to marry Edward, then I would suggest we work on accomplishing that first."

"But Edward hasn't even asked me."

"Only because he never believed he stood a chance of winning your hand."

She shook her head and lowered herself to the edge of her bed. "Edward is the finest gentleman there is."

"Agreed, but his yearly income won't be much to speak of. Papa will likely point this out and, if he chooses, use this argument to try and encourage you to make a different match."

"He's already told me that it would thrill him if I were to form an attachment with Cumberland."

Jack snorted. "Of course it would. The viscount is like a bloody champion race horse among a bunch of mules. Wealthy, titled, handsome, and young, he would be impossible for any man to compete with if he chose to offer for you."

"If my heart weren't otherwise engaged, I'd heartily agree, but how can I marry a man for money and position when I'm in love with someone else?"

"I've been asking myself a similar question lately, which is how I realized I need to act – stop Sophia from marrying Edward, ensure I marry her instead, and face whatever the outcome may be. At least she and I will be together. I know we'll be happy, even if Papa does cut me off and deny me my inheritance."

Felicity paled. "Deny you your inheritance? Jack what are you talking about? He cannot do that. The house is entailed so it has to go to you."

"The house yes, but not the funds."

Felicity narrowed her gaze and rose to her feet with stiff movements. "Are you telling me Papa has threatened to strike you from his will if you marry the woman of your choosing?"

Jack nodded. He'd not meant to reveal so much – had no desire for his own strained relationship with their father to impact his sister's. But years of bitterness and resentment bottled up inside him caused the words to pop out, unbidden. "It made me so bloody angry I could scarcely see straight."

"As well it should," Felicity said. She balled her hands into fists. "Papa has no right."

"On the contrary, he has every right. It's his money."

"That doesn't make it fair." She marched past him and flung her door open.

"Felicity, wait. Where are you going?"

"To give Papa a piece of my mind."

Jack's heart knocked against his chest. He rushed after her. "You mustn't. We need to think rationally about this." He caught her arm and forced her to stop. "The last time I acted in anger I nearly ruined everything."

Her jaw tightened as she gazed up at him with fiery eyes. "Then what's your plan?"

"To safeguard your future with Edward. Once that has been achieved, I'll marry Sophia."

"Even if it means giving up your inheritance?"

His lips quirked. "Of course. I could hardly claim to love her if I were unwilling to choose her above all else, now could I?"

Felicity scrunched her nose. "You're certain you don't want to fight for both?"

He shook his head. "I don't want to warn Papa of my intentions since doing so will provide him with the chance to stop me. So I'll take the risk of forfeiting my inheritance." When she gave him a worried look he said, "Sophia and I will be fine without it. After Papa issued his threat, I worked toward ensuring my independence so I'd have the freedom to do as I please. The returns I've made on my investments are substantial, Felicity. You mustn't concern yourself about that."

"Very well. If you're sure."

"I am." He glanced toward the hallway clock and noted the time. "Everyone will be heading downstairs for afternoon tea in another ten minutes, so we need to leave now if we're to avoid being detained."

"Leave and go where?"

"To the vicarage of course, so we can discuss our next move with Sophia and Edward."

Excitement flowed through his veins as he helped Felicity into the carriage. As reckless as his decision to circumvent his parents' approval on a matter that could impact all their lives, it was also liberating. For once, he felt free, like he'd cast off the shackles he'd worn since birth and escaped the rules that had governed his life thus far.

He gave the coachman directions and leapt in after his sister, eager to be on his way before anyone had a chance to stop them and ask where they were headed. With only two miles between Eastgate Abbey and the town of Ramcroft, they reached their destination swiftly.

Jack opened the door and alit, then handed Felicity down. Forcing a moderate pace even though he was tempted to race toward the front door, he tempered his impatience and guided Felicity calmly up the garden path.

"Ready?" he asked. When she nodded he reached for the knocker and gave the solid wood door three loud raps. His stomach fluttered and his heart raced. This was it. They were finally going to make things right – cement a plan and undo the mess he'd caused. Four people's happiness hung in the balance, his own included.

The Fenmore maid of all works named Gertrude answered his call. "The family's in the parlor with a visitor. I'm sure they'd be happy to have you both join them."

"This visitor," Jack inquired while he removed his hat and Felicity took off her bonnet. "Anyone we might know?"

"Possibly," Gertrude said. She took his hat and Felicity's bonnet and set the items aside on a table. "It's the Marquess of Maypoole. Recently arrived from London, from what I gather."

Jack stilled in the process of shucking his great-coat and met Felicity's gaze with a frown. Jack had encountered Maypoole at his club a few weeks prior, and although the two weren't friends, Jack had stopped to offer his condolences on the passing of Maypoole's father. It had been a brief conversation but the marquess had mentioned his intention to visit this corner of England soon and had promised to call at Eastgate when he did. Jack had not been aware of his acquaintance with the Fenmores though. Odd that.

Then again, if memory served, Mr. Fenmore had a distant cousin attached to some branch of the peerage, so maybe this was how they knew each other. He shrugged and hung his greatcoat on the coatrack, then helped Felicity do the same with her pelisse.

"Please show us in," he told Gertrude who promptly led them through to the parlor. Exhilaration bubbled through him with each step he took. He could scarcely wait to see Sophia again. Already it had been two days since he'd last spoken with her, which was much too long now that he knew she loved him as fiercely as he loved her.

Gertrude opened the parlor door and announced their arrival. "Lord Hawthorne and Miss Felicity have arrived." She stepped aside so Jack and his sister could enter the room.

"How good of you to join us," Mr. Fenmore said in an uncommonly strenuous tone. He immediately stood, as did Edward and Maypoole. All three men had been occupying various armchairs while enjoying tea with Mrs. Fenmore and Sophia who sat on the sofa. Mr. Fenmore gave the marquess a hasty look before returning his attention to Jack and his sister. He cleared his throat. "You are most welcome. Please, Miss Felicity, come have a seat."

Edward immediately gestured toward the chair he'd vacated, then offered Felicity his hand to help her into it while she greeted the rest of the occupants in the room. A few whispered words passed between them, Jack noted. A flush brightened Felicity's cheeks, instilling in him a certainty that she and Edward were indeed meant for each other.

He swept his gaze toward Sophia and instantly frowned in response to the startled look in her eyes. Was it just him, or did the atmosphere seem rather strained? Tempered by the awkward feeling of having intruded on an important meeting, he kept his attention on the woman he loved. "Miss Fenmore." He dipped his head in greeting, then quickly acknowledged her mother before giving his attention to Maypoole. "Welcome to Ramcroft, my lord. I trust your journey went well?"

"Indeed." Maypoole stiffly accepted the hand Jack offered and gave it a firm shake. "I had intended to come a bit sooner but then a complication arose with regard to my father's will. Apparently a cousin of his wished to contest part of it, but all of that has been cleared up now so here I am at last."

"I'm glad of it," Jack said even though he wasn't sure anyone else felt the same. It was awfully hard to gauge their emotions.

"Thank you." Maypoole's expression grew somber. "My father has everything to do with it. Turns out, he had quite the confession to make on his death bed."

"Oh?" Jack accepted the cup and saucer Mrs. Fenmore gave him and took a quick sip. Perfect.

"Apparently, my brother and I are not his only children." Maypoole's eyes darkened. His lips flattened into a hard line. "My mother perished in childbirth while my brother and I were away at Eton."

"I'm sorry," Jack told him.

Maypoole's answering snort surprised him. "According to what we were told, the child – a daughter – died from influenza a few months after. Only that wasn't true. My father just couldn't stand to be near the person who'd taken the love of his life from him. So as soon as the infant outgrew her wet nurse, he travelled with her to these parts, placed her in a basket, and left her inside the church for strangers to find. Thankfully the agent I hired to track her down has proven to be a competent fellow."

Jack froze, the tea he'd just drunk like a lump of lead lodged in his throat. He stared at Maypoole, then at Sophia, and once again at Maypoole while the enormity of what had just been revealed sank in. Sophia the orphan, daughter of only God knew who for most of her life, was a marquess's sister?

"I still don't understand how he managed it," Mrs. Fenmore said. "There must have been questions. Did you not suspect anything?"

Maypoole shook his head, his expression somber. When he spoke, bitterness laced every word. "Like I said, my brother and I were absent. Rather than returning home that year for the holidays, our father came to collect us. He said he had to escape the memories crowding him at every turn – that he needed to spend some time with us alone, away from it all. We had no cause to doubt him. As for the servants, those in senior positions were fiercely loyal to him. As proven by the fact that his valet was able to make his voice crack whenever he mentioned my father's struggle to keep my poor sister alive. Knowing the truth – how unjustly he treated her – is eating at my very soul." His eyes clouded with deep regret. "I have to make this right."

Jack's stomach tightened, then unclenched as his shock subsided. Although the deception clearly angered Maypoole, this was actually excellent news – the best he'd had in years. For if it were true, then there really was no reason for him not to marry Sophia. His father would no longer have any cause to object. Which meant they could have it all – the happily ever after they wanted and the inheritance he would have had to give up otherwise. Not to mention that he'd avoid the potential scandal he might have faced if he married a woman with no connections.

Maypoole took a deep breath. "Naturally, I have no wish to break up what looks to be a happy family. My intention is not to insist Sophia leave the home she has known all her life or the people who have been kind enough to love her. But as my sister, she will have certain privileges. For the sake of establishing these, I'd like to make her existence known to the peerage. Officially, that is."

"Thank you, my lord," Mr. Fenmore said with marked hesitation. "You are…most generous."

"I am merely attempting to right a terrible wrong," Maypoole said. He shifted his gaze toward Sophia. "I am terribly sorry for what has happened, Sophia."

"It's quite all right." The strain in Sophia's features suggested it would take time for her to adjust to Maypoole's news. Yet to Jack's amazement, she faced her brother with gentle dignity. "If it hadn't, I never would have met the Fenmores, and I can assure you, my lord, that I am most grateful I did."

"To be certain, you were better off in their care than you ever would have been in my father's." Maypoole sighed. "If you wish to visit any of the family estates, you and the Fenmores are welcome there any time. My carriages are at your disposal and as of this moment, I shall be bestowing a monthly allowance on you. Furthermore, I'd like to plan your entrance into London Society this coming spring. As my newly discovered sister, you'll have some mystery attached to your name. This will undoubtedly aid your popularity, most notably with regard to encouraging suitors."

Jack blinked. This new situation, which had begun as a pleasant surprise, was starting to snowball out of control. If he didn't say something soon, he might lose the reins on it altogether. He turned to Maypoole, who'd always struck him as a sensible fellow. "Before you proceed any further, my lord, I wonder if it might be possible for me to have a word with you in private?"

Surprise caused Maypoole's eyes to flicker. He stared at Jack just long enough to suggest he'd like to conclude his business regarding Sophia first and that he found Jack's interruption frustrating. But as the gentleman he was and, Jack reasoned, in deference to his position as an earl's heir, Maypoole dipped his head in agreement. "Very well."

"May we make use of your study, Mr. Fenmore?" Jack asked.

"By all means." In spite of his easy tone, deep grooves were present on Mr. Fenmore's brow. Clearly the man was concerned over Jack's unusual request. Jack couldn't fault him when they'd all been deep in a conversation that had by all accounts been moving along with great promise.

Edward, on the other hand, who'd remained at Felicity's shoulder since she'd claimed his seat, offered Jack a nod of encouragement as Jack turned for the door.

"You are aware that this request of yours to speak with me in private when I was in the middle of laying out ways in which I hope to improve Sophia's life may not only be construed as rude but highly suspicious." Maypoole stepped inside Mr. Fenmore's study, shut the door, and crossed his arm. "I hope your reason for it is sound."

"It is." Jack faced the marquess with steel in his spine. Maypoole was ten years his senior – seventeen years older than Sophia. They'd never run with the same crowd. Indeed, the marquess had always struck Jack as the somber sort who never engaged in anything fun. Which prompted Jack to wonder how his wife, a lovely lady with a tremendously outgoing personality, tolerated him. He cleared his throat. "Since you mentioned sponsoring a Season for Sophia, I thought it best to tell you that she and I intend to marry."

Maypoole's brows dipped. "According to what Mr. Fenmore has told me, she was engaged to his son until they broke things off last night."

Relief swam through Jack's veins. He'd not had a chance to inquire how things stood between Sophia and Edward – if they had spoken and come to a mutual agreement. He was glad to know they had. Hopefully, Edward's parents did not begrudge them this decision and all would be well in the end.

"Which they did because Mr. Edward Fenmore would rather marry my sister Felicity while Sophia wishes to marry me. She and I love each other, my lord."

"Then why, if I may ask, did she wind up engaged to another man?"

Jack gave Maypoole a swift account of the facts, then added, "As I'm sure you can appreciate, I needed to secure an income and a viable path forward if I was to thwart my father and marry Sophia. This took time. Mistakes were made, I'll grant you. She didn't know until now that my heart beats for her and her alone. Truth is, I didn't realize it either until I returned and found her attached. As a result, she lost hope, and since she did not believe she had many prospects, she accepted the offer of marriage she received."

"Yes, but how did…" Moorland waved his hand. "Never mind. I doubt it matters and even if it does, I've little desire to try and comprehend the intricacies of this mess you've created. So, let's focus on the facts at hand. You wish to marry Sophia, yes?"

"I do."

"And if what you say is true, she wishes to marry you as well?"

"If you doubt me, you may ask her yourself."

Maypoole smirked. "Fear not, Hawthorne, for I intend to do precisely that, I can assure you. But if she is willing, then I suppose a marriage would be possible. Technically speaking. After all, now that she has connections, I doubt your father will keep protesting the match. Which should allow you to retain the inheritance you stood to lose while also avoiding the possible scandal of him cutting you off."

"My thought exactly."

"By the by," Maypoole said, "I do commend you for trying to make your own way – for fighting for what you wanted by creating your own fortune. I respect you for it, truly I do. However…"

Jack braced himself. Unease stroked his spine.

"I'm inclined to believe my sister can do better."

"I beg your pardon?"

"Your reputation is practically in the gutter. You're a reputed rake. Indeed, it's near impossible to read a paper without seeing your name in the gossip column."

"I'll admit there have been some indiscretions."

"Some?" Maypoole snorted. "Point is I value my good name too much to have it tarnished in any way, as would likely occur if you became my brother-in-law. I also worry about my sister's future. After everything my family put her through, I feel it's my duty to give her the best chance of success I possibly can. So I'm sorry, but I shall have to oppose this match."

Jack stared at the marquess. A violent haze of red descended upon his vision. Heat shot up his spine and into his skull. He leaned toward the opposing force standing before him and balled his hands into fists. "No."

Maypoole raised one arrogant brow. "No?"

"You will not have a say in this matter. I refuse to allow it."

"You refuse to allow it? Ha!"

"Test me if you must," Jack persisted. "In any way you choose. Allow me to prove my worth or so help me, I'll challenge you here and now. One thing is certain, I will not let one more person ruin my life, or hers."

"From where I stand, I just improved her life greatly," Maypoole drawled with irritating smugness. "But I would hate to have a duel forced upon me, so let's see..."

Jack held his breath while Maypoole seemed to consider the options. Eventually, the marquess narrowed his gaze and stared straight into Jack's eyes with unyielding force. "You will have to grovel, beg Society's forgiveness for your rakish ways, and ensure the papers don't mention your name for one full year. At the end of which, I'll reconsider your request to marry my sister."

"You can't be serious."

"And don't even think of eloping or ruining her to force my hand," Maypoole added. "Or I will make certain your family suffers the consequence."

"But if you're giving Sophia a season then..." Jack swallowed. "Then she will attract attention. Gentlemen will vie for her hand."

"And she may choose one of them instead. One never knows what it will take to turn a young woman's head. And since you need to stay out of the papers, you'll not be able to attend."

It took every effort Jack possessed to hide his

sudden contempt for the marquess. How dare he do this to him and Sophia? How dare he swoop in out of nowhere and lay claim to both their futures? It was beyond the pale. Outrageous and unfair. But since his foe was a powerful man who could easily follow through on his threat, Jack saw no way out. So he stuck out his hand and waited for Maypoole to clasp it.

"I agree to your terms, my lord."

Maypoole smiled as he shook Jack's hand. A bitter taste slid over Jack's tongue. It felt like he'd just made a deal with the devil. The only thing that lifted his spirits later was the kiss Sophia gave him in the Fenmore garden once Maypoole was gone. They'd stepped outside, partly to give Felicity and Edward a chance to reveal their intentions to the Fenmores in private, but also so they could be alone.

Jack wrapped his arms around Sophia and held her close, dreading the moment when they'd have to part. "This is quite a change for you."

"I still can't believe it," she said. "It's so unexpected."

"But a welcome surprise?"

"Only in the sense that it makes things easier for you and me."

Jack smoothed his thumb over her cheek. "Sophia, Maypoole has stipulations."

She frowned at him. "What do you mean?"

He took a deep breath and told her, ensuring he

left nothing out. Her features hardened with every word he spoke, and when he was done, her hands had balled into fists. "He cannot do this, Jack."

"Of course he can, but at least he's willing to give us a chance – to give me a chance to truly win you." He pushed a stray lock of hair behind her ear. "Promise me you won't fall in love with anyone else."

A gorgeous smile brightened her eyes until they sparkled. "There will never be anyone else, Jack. I will wait for you as long as it takes."

Bolstered by her words, Jack pressed his mouth to hers, imparting in his kiss all that was in his heart and the dream he had of a future with her by his side.

CHAPTER NINE

Eastgate Hall. One year later, to the day.

Trepidation hugged Jack's shoulders as he oversaw the preparations underway in the ballroom. Footmen were standing on ladders so they could hang garlands wrapped in ropes of crystal beads intended to make them shimmer. In the adjacent room where supper would be served, centerpieces made from pine, holly, and mistletoe, all adorned with pinecones and ribbons, were being distributed on each table.

"I see you're keeping busy," Kaitlin said. She and her husband, Mr. Irving, had arrived three days earlier and had both helped Jack make the decorations. "It's coming together nicely."

Jack nodded. He wanted it to be perfect, so he'd not just seen to collecting all the things required, had not simply supervised the servants as they strung together the pine and tied pretty bows. No, he'd seen to each and every detail, threading beads on string himself and showing everyone how he wanted things done. The result was exactly what he'd hoped for and he could not deny being proud.

"I'm glad you're here," he told his sister. He'd not seen much of her since she'd married, but he liked the man she'd picked for her husband. He seemed to dote on Kaitlin and had not been able to contain his obvious excitement when they'd arrived and informed the family they now expected their first child.

"Me too," Kaitlin said. She moved in closer to Jack and leaned her head against his shoulder. "It's a wonder how much things can change in a year. I still can't believe Felicity has a daughter."

Jack smiled. He'd escorted Kaitlin and Irving to Norham where Felicity and Edward now lived. The small parish was nearly twenty miles east of Ramcroft, but from what Jack gathered, Edward and Felicity were incredibly happy. Their daughter, Amanda, the loveliest one-month-old baby Jack had ever laid eyes on, had held a special place in his heart since the moment he'd met her. She'd also increased his yearning for a family of his own.

All the more reason for him to make certain the ball tomorrow evening would be a smashing success.

"I know what I'm about to say next might make you angry but—"

"Then don't say it," he told Kaitlin, his muscles already tensing in preparation for the subject he feared she would broach.

"Jack." She straightened and moved so she stood before him, blocking his view of the ballroom and forcing his attention upon her. "You need to make peace with Papa."

"No."

"I agree he was overly harsh with you. No one is disputing that he has treated you most unfairly. Not even Mama. But having the two of you refuse to speak to one another is creating a very awkward atmosphere for the rest of us. It's not the sort of environment I want my own children to grow up in."

"Then it is fortunate for you that you do not live here anymore."

"I rather agree with you there, but what of christenings, birthdays, and Christmases? We've never been especially close as a family, so I think it would be nice for us to make more of an effort in that regard. Irving's parents arrange a yearly get together where everyone is invited. I'd like for us to do the same, though it will require your being able to be in the same room as Papa without looking as though you want to murder him."

"He has cut me off and denied me my inheritance, Kaitlin." In the aftermath of his conversation with Maypoole last year, Jack had returned home incensed. In his anger, he'd forgotten himself and had muttered something about regretting he'd not eloped with Sophia before the marquess arrived. The revelation that Jack had intended to thwart Papa's wishes and marry Sophia in secret had made Papa so bloody mad he'd altered his will that same evening and hadn't talked to Jack since.

To say the situation this past year had been difficult would be a great understatement. Jack couldn't run to London this time. He had to stay out of the papers if he was to win Sophia. Which meant he could not afford being mentioned in any capacity, not even as a guest attending a musicale. So he'd remained at Eastgate, ever conscious of his father's presence in other parts of the house.

At least in the beginning, he'd still had Felicity, Kaitlin, and Sophia. But then Felicity had married Edward and moved out. Kaitlin had followed suit shortly after. And in March, Sophia had gone off to London for her Season, after which Jack had experienced loneliness like never before.

Even though he'd kept himself busy helping the locals make necessary repairs to their homes, it hadn't been the same. The moment Sophia left, she took his heart with her, leaving behind a wide, gaping hole too large for the letters she wrote him to fill.

Only his mother kept his spirits up. They'd walked together and visited with the Fenmores twice a week. She'd tell him that the year would be over before he knew it and that he must keep his mind on his goal. He'd cursed Maypoole, but his mother had been the one to convince him the marquess wasn't entirely wrong. Sophia deserved a respectable husband and as such, Jack ought to do his best to come up to scratch.

Still, his father's decision had been a blow. Not because Jack cared about the money. He'd been prepared to give it all up for Sophia when he'd thought she lacked connections and that was the price he must pay. But for Papa to deny him everything anyway, not because of something Jack had done, but because of a mere idea, angered him like nothing else. Clearly it angered Papa as well, for he'd been the one to walk away and slam the door in Jack's face.

"I cannot be the one to apologize." Jack held Kaitlin's gaze. "I'm sorry, but he ought to beg my forgiveness, not the other way around."

"Everyone agrees, but I fear his pride will never permit him to do so."

"Then I suppose we shall remain estranged for the rest of our lives, Kaitlin. I'm sorry."

She answered with a sad smile but rather than force the issue any further, she said, "It will be lovely to see Sophia again when she and the Maypooles get here."

Jack cast a glance toward the windows and expelled a breath when he saw that the weather was holding. With only a gentle breeze and a few stray clouds, the Maypoole carriage ought to arrive unhindered.

"Do you suppose she'll be different from when we last saw her?" Kaitlin asked.

Jack frowned. He hadn't considered such a possibility. "I don't know. The reports I received from my friends, the Earl of Fielding and the Earl of Yates, have given me no cause to think so. But then, neither of them knew her before she became Maypoole's sister."

"You asked them to keep an eye on her?"

"I did," Jack confessed. Both men had married two years ago and were deeply in love with their wives. They understood the pain Jack felt over being parted from Sophia and the angst he experienced at not being there to protect her himself. Naturally, they were invited to attend his Christmas ball too, along with the neighboring gentry and any peers who desired to make the trip and were willing to stay at the two local inns the area offered. Eastgate Abbey itself was already full.

"There's no need to worry, you know." The edge of Kaitlin's mouth lifted. When Jack raised an eyebrow in question it turned into a full-fledged smile. "She's going to say yes, Jack. Sophia will be your wife before the year is done."

"Don't say that. I'll not have you tempting fate."

She rolled her eyes and laughed, prompting Jack's

heart to beat a faster rhythm. It wouldn't be long now. Sophia would be here soon.

As wonderful as it had been to go to London and be introduced at court, to dine with dukes and duchesses and receive the attentions of titled lords and wealthy gentlemen alike, none of it compared to the thrill Sophia experienced as the carriage she travelled in rolled up the driveway toward Eastgate Abbey. The conveyance rocked to a halt, the steps were set down, and the door opened by a footman. Lord Maypoole alit first. He turned and helped his wife, a woman Sophia had taken a great liking to, before offering Sophia his assistance.

Her toes had barely touched the ground before Eastgate's front door opened and Kaitlin rushed out onto the driveway with squeals of delight. Sophia grinned in response to her friend's warm welcome and swiftly made the necessary introductions. She was just finishing when she noticed Jack. He must have followed his sister outside but refrained from a similar display of affection. Instead, he stood completely still, hands clasped behind his back, his dark eyes fixed upon her as if he'd been adrift and had just found his anchor.

The ache she'd experienced when they'd last parted returned, not with a deep sense of loss this time, but rather with the burning need to throw herself into his arms. Instead, she held herself in check and gave him a smile. Her world had been turned upside down this past year, especially by her brother's stipulations. She understood them, as irritating as it was, and would not urge Jack to ruin their chances of marriage by being reckless at the last moment.

"Welcome to Eastgate Abbey," Jack said, addressing his newly arrived guests as a whole. The edge of his mouth lifted and when he spoke again, his voice was softer. "You look well, Sophia, and lovelier than I recall. Which I'd not have thought possible."

His words, so fondly spoken, seeped beneath her skin and warmed her soul. The blush she could feel in her cheeks was unavoidable. No one had ever affected her as Jack did.

"Please." Jack swept his arm toward the front door. "Let's go inside."

Kaitlin led the way, allowing Jack to approach Sophia. He offered her his arm, which she readily accepted, and together they followed the others.

"I've missed you desperately," he murmured as they climbed the steps. Behind them, the footmen could be heard unloading the luggage.

"And I you," she whispered. "Thank God our wait is almost over."

"Agreed." He squeezed her arm. "We need only be a little more patient."

They entered the abbey where the butler helped them all remove their outerwear. And then two maids were showing the Maypooles and Sophia up to their respective rooms. A glance over her shoulder confirmed Jack remained in the foyer, quietly watching her climb the stairs. Her heart hammered wildly against her breast as her gaze caught his. The ball tomorrow evening could not arrive soon enough.

A knock sounded at Jack's bedchamber door the following evening. Standing before his cheval glass, his valet, Jones, was in the process of helping him on with his jacket.

"Come in," Jack called.

His mother entered, dressed in a lovely green gown she'd ordered specifically for tonight's occasion. "You look remarkably handsome."

"And you look exceptionally lovely, Mama. That color suits you to perfection."

Mama smiled. "I brought the item you asked for." She placed a tiny box on top of his dresser. "Sophia is the best choice you could have made in a wife. I've always thought so."

"A pity Papa doesn't agree," Jack muttered. He thanked Jones and dismissed him.

"Your father can have some firm opinions. He can be stubborn and difficult. But at the end of the day, he loves you, Jack, and this rift between the two of you is hurting him."

Jack snorted. "I seriously doubt that."

"Please. Talk to him."

"After he cut me out of his will for daring to love someone he thought unfit to be his daughter-in-law?"

"You know it's not because of that." Mama pressed her lips together. "He's waiting for you in his study and he's ready to talk. If I were you, I'd swallow my pride and take this opportunity to mend your differences." When Jack simply stared at her, she added, "It will give your new life with Sophia the proper start it deserves, without all this negativity hanging over your head."

Phrased like that, Jack had to admit there might be a point to making amends with his father. Even if he had to be the one to start the process. Lord, how he loathed the idea of doing so. "Fine."

Her eyes lit up. "Thank you and good luck."

Jack blew out a breath and picked up the box she'd brought. He placed it securely in his jacket pocket and followed her into the hallway. According to the clock in the foyer, the guests would be arriving in half an hour. And since most of those he'd invited had accepted his invitation, he expected a large crowd.

When he and his mother reached the door to his father's study, Jack dropped a kiss on her cheek. "I'll see you soon."

Then, with his heart in his throat, he entered the one room he'd not set foot in for a full year. He scanned the space and found his father standing with his back toward him near the window, drink in hand. Jack cleared his throat. "Mama said I might find you here."

Papa turned, his features carefully schooled as always. "She threatened to leave me unless I agreed to speak with you."

A startled laugh escaped Jack's lips. "Did she really?"

Papa fixed his gaze on Jack's. "I believe she called me an unreasonable curmudgeon."

Jack raised an eyebrow. "I'm shocked."

A hint of humor flickered in Papa's gaze. His lips twitched. "Truth is, she's not wrong. It's just been so damn hard for me to figure out what to say. I was so incredibly angry with you when you told me you'd planned on running away – of marrying behind my back."

"You didn't really leave me much choice. If you'll recall, you did threaten to cut me off and strike me from your will if I married Sophia. You told me a woman like her could never be more than my mistress." Jack took a deep breath and tried to cast off the anger that once again gripped him. "With this in mind, I feared you'd try and stop a potential wedding if you heard of our plan."

Papa bowed his head with a sigh. He looked defeated. "I was wrong to say what I did. Sophia's a lovely girl. I've always thought so. But I had this family's reputation to consider. I worried what strangers would think and the impact such a union might have on Kaitlin and Felicity."

"You weren't wrong to be concerned," Jack said. "But you were wrong to punish me for something I never ended up doing."

"I know." Papa raised his gaze to Jack's. "Please forgive me."

The words were so simple and yet they'd been one long year in the making.

Jack's chest contracted in response. His throat tightened.

"Of course," he managed, then crossed the distance between them and gave his father a hug. When he stepped back, Papa's eyes had grown suspiciously bright and shiny. "Come now, let's go and greet our guests."

Papa nodded and swallowed the last of his drink. "I trust you're ready for your big night?"

"Indeed," Jack assured him. "I've never been more ready for anything else in my life."

CHAPTER TEN

SINCE HER ARRIVAL in the ballroom nearly one hour earlier, Sophia had greeted several guests, most of whom she knew from London. There were the Earl and Countess of Yates, the Earl and Countess of Fielding, the Duke and Duchess of Huntley, the Duke and Duchess of Coventry, the Duke and Duchess of Redding, Redding's brother Mr. Lowell and his wife, Mrs. Lowell, along with the notorious Duke of Windham – the former Scoundrel of St. Giles – and his duchess.

According to the gossip Sophia had managed to pick up, all of these peers had made unconventional matches. The Duke of Huntley, for instance, had been no more than a bare-knuckle fighter raised in the slums until circumstance had launched him into the midst of the *ton*. His sisters had since become the duchesses of Coventry and Redding. And then there was Jack's friend Fielding who'd married a woman whose father had been condemned for treason.

Essentially, each and every one of these people had struggled to find their happily ever after, just like Sophia and Jack. She related to them and liked them all the more for their decisions to turn their backs on social expectation and make their own rules.

"Have you seen Jack?" she asked when she met with Felicity and Kaitlin. Both were accompanied by their husbands with whom they'd just danced a quadrille.

The sisters glanced at each other and Felicity said, "Not since he greeted us at the door."

Sophia bit her lip and craned her neck for a better view of the room, only there were too many people milling about, and she wasn't nearly tall enough to spot the man she sought.

"I'm sure he'll find you as soon as he's able," Kaitlin told her.

Sophia wrinkled her nose. Since her arrival yesterday afternoon, she'd scarcely seen him at all. He'd vanished by the time she'd finished settling in and returned downstairs, and had remained absent when she'd set out with his mother to visit the Fenmores. Her only glimpse of him occurred during last night's dinner, after which he'd once again made himself scarce.

Considering how eager she'd been to return and

spend time with him once more, she had to admit she was rather disappointed by his seeming lack of enthusiasm.

"Perhaps you'd care to dance with me while you wait?" Edward asked.

Sophia forced a smile she didn't quite feel and accepted his invitation. They approached the dance floor, only to halt and glance around when no new tune commenced. It seemed they weren't the only ones wondering over the musicians' sudden silence, the three violinists all standing about as if they'd no intention of playing any more.

How odd.

Sophia frowned and turned to Edward. "What do you suppose is going on?"

"I think you're about to find out," Edward said with a grin.

Turning, Sophia looked in the same direction as Edward and gasped. Because there Jack was, his dark eyes fixed upon her with such intensity she felt the heat of his gaze all the way to her bones. Heavens, he was handsome, and lord help her if he did not possess the ability to make her go up in flames. She needed a fan. Desperately.

"Esteemed guests," Jack began, "I am honored to welcome you all to this Yuletide fete at Eastgate Abbey. Some of you have journeyed far in order to be here, for which I and the rest of my family thank you. And since you are here, you'll have the chance to bear witness to something I doubt you ever imagined you'd see."

Sophia stilled, her every nerve on keen alert. She glanced to her right and caught her brother's eye, relief spilling through her when he met her gaze with approval. This was it – Jack's big moment – his chance to make everything right. If he pulled it off as he'd promised he would, Maypoole would let them marry.

Around her, the room came alive with whispers as guests began placing wagers on what might occur.

"The redemption of a rake," Jack said, a glint of devilish charm in his eyes. "Tonight you shall watch a rogue humble himself before your very eyes. And you will be given the power to grant him forgiveness. Or to deny it."

Claps and cheers resounded, shaking the air.

Sophia swallowed. She'd known Jack had to make a grand gesture, but she'd not realized how daring it would be until he placed their fate in everyone else's hands. Jack had a reputation after all, and it wasn't a good one. In fact, she'd learned just how ill-reputed he was while in London when she'd overheard a scandalous conversation between two married women. They'd mentioned a craving for *strawberries dipped in champagne*, which as it turned out, had not referred to the fruit or the drink, but rather to the manner in which Jack seduced. They'd given it its own name!

She tried not to think of that – of all the women who'd come before her. What did it matter? She was the one he loved, and if she'd ever been in doubt, he'd proven himself this past year with the sacrifice he'd made.

"Now, allow me to make my pledge," Jack said, his voice cutting through the din. He spread out his arms like some dark and dangerous angel in search of acceptance, and holding her gaze, he dropped to one knee. A buzz of excitement swept through the crowd. Sophia's pulse leapt in response to the blood rushing through her veins. "I, Jack Nathaniel Lancaster, beg your pardon for my sins. I've been a cad, a scoundrel, a good for nothing debaucher. Please hear me repent.

"I swear to you I have cast off my wicked ways and that I shall never again take a woman to bed unless she's my lawfully wedded wife. And if I ever give you cause to think I've strayed from this oath, then you shall be honor bound to have me flogged."

Sophia parted her lips in shock.

Jack's eyes blazed with relentless intensity. "Can you forgive me so I may make peace with my past and lay claim to the future I so dearly want?"

A hesitation followed. Sophia could scarcely breathe. There was an intolerable silence, during which she believed she might shatter if she tried to move. And then, just when she feared all was lost, the room exploded with cheers and applause. Whistles pierced the air as wild shouts rose to the ceiling. Sophia glanced at Maypoole and saw he was clapping. A distinct smile of approval curved his lips. His wife said something to him, prompting him to nod in Sophia's direction.

That was all it took for her to rush toward Jack, who'd just managed to rise by the time she flung her arms around his neck and hugged him with all her might. He swept one arm about her waist and grinned. "I feared I'd overdone it for a moment."

"It was perfect, Jack, just perfect."

"I've yet to have your brother's consent, but if he grants it, will you agree to be my wife, Sophia?"

"Of course."

He gazed into her eyes and the connection that had always existed between them tightened. "I have loved you forever and this past year without you has been a hell unlike any other."

"I rather feel the same way, which is why I would recommend that we move this proposal along so we can get married as soon as possible."

"I think that can be arranged." Maypoole's voice rumbled next to Sophia's right shoulder. "My wife and I wish you both happy."

Jack's grin broadened as he pulled a small box from his jacket pocket and flipped it open to reveal a gold band adorned by diamonds. He took the ring and slipped it onto Sophia's finger, then lowered his mouth and kissed her, right there in the middle of the overcrowded ballroom.

Fortunately, in spite of the unpredictable weather one might expect in late December, the sun shone on the day of Sophia and Jack's wedding. Frost clinging to tree branches shimmered, the clear sky added a bright splash of blue, and the air – crisp with the promise of new beginnings – was wonderfully invigorating, though perhaps a bit chilly.

Sophia didn't mind. She was far too happy to notice the cold. Especially during the ride to London after the wedding breakfast had been concluded. She'd happily snuggled up to Jack while he held her close in his arms.

Now, alone with him in the bedchamber they would share at the townhouse where he'd made his home before Maypoole forced him to stay away from London, Sophia enjoyed a glass of champagne while admiring the furnishings.

"You're welcome to redecorate if you like," Jack said. He stood near the fireplace, watching her with inquisitive eyes.

"Thank you, but that won't be necessary, Jack. I actually love what you've done. You have excellent taste."

A smile formed upon his lips. "As proven by my decision to marry you."

Heat flooded her cheeks. She took a sip of her cool drink and savored the fruity flavor. Her gaze met his and the air shifted, crackling slightly with increased awareness. He set his glass aside and silently held out his hand. Sophia's pulse leapt and her skin tightened over her shoulders. She took one step toward him and then another, ever aware of his darkening eyes. Her stomach fluttered, a shiver swept down her spine, and then she was in his arms. A sigh of pleasure escaped her throat the second before his mouth met hers.

Since their engagement, she and Jack had managed to sneak the occasional kiss, but none were as perfect or passionate as this. This one could be enjoyed without restriction, without ever having to end unless they wished for it to, and was destined to lead to more.

Jack's fingers found hers and gently removed the glass from her hand. It made a soft clink as he set it aside, his mouth never leaving hers. And then his arms came fully around her. His hands pressed her flush up against him. A gasp of surprise parted her lips and he immediately took advantage.

Solid and strong, Jack held her while kissing her breathless. His capable hands coaxed a wanton response from her body, instilling in her a craving for increased contact, fewer clothes, and something so primal she feared she'd go mad if she were denied it. Desperate, she raked her fingers through his black hair, heedless of the whimpers she heard herself make. This was Jack. She'd known him all her life and she would not be embarrassed by her love or her want for him.

Her fingers moved to his cravat, untying and pulling until it came free. It was as if the action undid the restraint he'd placed on himself for he suddenly growled and roughly began unfastening her gown while kicking off his shoes. Frenzied movements followed, heightened by a shared need to bring their union to its climax before they perished from hunger. He helped her remove his jacket and shirt while dragging her gown away from her body. Frantic fingers tugged at her stays until they were carelessly flung aside. Her chemise and stockings soon followed along with the rest of his clothes.

Jack pressed his mouth hard against hers as he scooped her up in his arms and carried her to the bed. He followed her down, his added weight pressing her into the mattress. Sophia dug her fingertips into his broad back and marveled at the resistance of his lean body. Apparently, her husband was made of incredibly hard muscle.

"Sophia," he murmured, gentling the kiss while trailing one hand down over her hip. "My wife and lifelong friend. I love you so much my heart aches."

His sweet words brushed over her skin, the warmth of them curling their way around her until she was filled to the brim with joy. Reaching up, she cupped his cheek, the light stubble abrading her skin in a strangely delicious way. "I love you too, Jack. With every fiber of my being."

His eyes held hers, locking her to him, before he lowered his mouth once more and kissed her as if he were starving. He loved her with his mouth, his every touch, and gentle caresses. And as they joined, Sophia hugged him to her and savored the moment. Because this was where she belonged. It was where she had *always* belonged.

Ready for another story? Check out ***Mr. Donahue's Total Surrender!***

And sign up for my newsletter at www.sophiebarnes.com so you don't miss out on my freebies, special deals, and giveaways. You'll receive a complimentary copy of **No Ordinary Duke** with your subscription!

Did you enjoy **The Roguish Baron**? If so, please take a moment to leave a review since this can help other readers discover books they'll love.

But wait! There's more!

Turn the page to keep reading.

Sneak peek coming up!
Keep reading for an excerpt from
Mr. Donahue's Total Surrender
An Enterprising Scoundrels novella

CHAPTER ONE

London, 1849

CALISTA FAULKNER CLASPED her hands together to keep from fidgeting. Her heart was in her throat. Goodness. She needed this position. Desperately.

Her stomach clenched at that thought. An employer might think her agitation signaled a lack of inexperience. And they'd be right.

She took a deep breath. Forced herself to sit still. After all, she'd not worked a single day in her life. But she was willing to learn, even though she feared she wouldn't be given the chance. Not after being turned away from eight businesses already, as well as an upper class home in need of a governess.

Seated across from her now in this neatly furnished office was yet another man with the power to determine her fate. He'd introduced himself as Mr. Greene, the Hotel Imperial's manager. She'd told him she was Jane Smith for the sake of preserving her anonymity.

It wouldn't do for her real name to get out.

Slim of build with thinning brown hair slicked

back, a slender nose, flat mouth, and beady eyes framed by wire-rimmed spectacles, Mr. Greene looked to be in his mid to late fifties.

"Frankly," he said, glancing at the pocket watch he'd placed on his desk, "I don't know what you mean to accomplish here without a letter of reference."

"I was hoping I might be permitted to prove myself capable," Calista said. She added a smile even though he proceeded to scowl. "My accounting skills are impeccable and—"

He stopped her with a snort. "Perhaps if you were to lower your expectations, you'd have more success in gaining employment."

"Right." Calista stared across at him with determination. "I also know what's required of a good maid and"—she swallowed when his eyebrows rose toward his hairline—"I can assure you I shall work hard to live up to the standards this hotel is known for."

"Hmm... You strike me as rather well-spoken. Educated even." Mr. Greene tilted his head while he studied her. She tried to sit perfectly still. "And your accent... American, is it?"

She nodded. "I'm from New York."

"Ah. Well thank you for coming in, Miss Smith. I wish you the best of luck in your...ahem...future endeavors."

Calista blinked. "So you're not hiring me?"

"No."

"Because I don't have references or because I'm American?"

Mr. Greene glanced at the door as if he hoped she'd decide to use it. "To be honest, it's both, but if it makes you feel any better I'd made up my mind before I learned where you're from."

Calista frowned. "Before I even spoke?"

A red hue colored Mr. Greene's cheeks. "While your proposal to work as maid is not entirely ridiculous, I fear you're too pretty. Wives won't trust you to clean their rooms. In case the husband sees you, that is. Again, I'm sorry."

Appalled by his implication that she might tempt a married man to stray, Calista stood, hands fisted at her sides. "Mr. Greene. All I want is honest work and while I may not have experience, I know how to make a bed and how to sweep a floor. Indeed, I'm even able to light a fire if that's what's required of me. These tasks are simple to do. They don't require much skill. As for my looks, they cannot be helped though I must say I disagree with your assessment. I'm not the sort of woman any wife need fear, and the fact that you would suggest as much is offensive to me. That aside, I swear to you that if you give me a chance, you won't be sorry." She took a deep breath and sank back onto her seat. Determined to make one final attempt, she leaned forward and said in earnest, "Please. I need this position."

"While I appreciate your fortitude, you simply aren't suited to work here, Miss Smith. Now please, if you don't mind, this interview is—"

The door opened behind Calista and someone else entered the room.

"A word please, Mr. Greene," a man's voice spoke from behind her.

Mr. Greene scrambled from his chair and crossed the floor. Calista twisted in her seat in an effort to catch a glimpse of the man who'd commanded, rather than asked, Mr. Greene to join him. He was gone from view before she had the chance.

Mr. Greene vanished as well. The door closed and a muted conversation ensued from the opposite side. What on earth was going on? It sounded like there might be some sort of emergency.

She was still trying to work her way through the various reasons for the stranger's interruption when Mr. Greene returned.

He stood for a moment in the doorway, watching her as though she were a riddle he didn't know how to solve.

"Well, Miss Smith," he finally said, "it seems you have a job."

Her jaw dropped. Had he not just dismissed her? She stared at Mr. Greene. Who was this man who'd spoken to him and what had he said to change his mind?

"If you still desire to work here you'll start as a scullery maid in the kitchen."

A scullery maid?

"But—"

"Take it or leave it, Miss Smith." When she didn't respond right away he said, "The pay isn't bad. You'll get ten pounds per annum, which is more than the position is worth, if you ask me."

Calista sank against her chair. At this rate, it would take forever before she'd have enough money to purchase a ticket back to New York.

"What about room and board?" she asked, hoping to avoid the cost of lodging so she could save more of her salary.

"There's nothing left in the servants' quarters, but I'm sure we can set up a cot for you in the pantry. As long as you're willing to clear it away each morning before you start."

Calista swallowed. This wasn't what she wanted for herself, but she couldn't afford to turn down the offer either. Not when she was running dangerously low on funds. Already, she'd been forced to sell most of the fine dresses she'd brought with her to England. If she refused the position, she'd likely end up on the street. Acquiring a job had proven hard enough without letting pride get in her way.

"Thank you, Mr. Greene." She would be polite and respectful, just as her mother had taught her. Calista stood, reticule in hand. "I'll just collect my things from the boarding house. It's not far, so I shan't be long."

Mr. Greene looked down his nose at her. "When you return, make sure you use the back entrance. The one on the side is reserved for the upstairs staff."

Calista forced a smile. "Duly noted."

When Mr. Greene stared back at her with both eyebrows raised, she bobbed a quick curtsey and took her leave.

One hour later, Calista Faulkner was handed a tub filled with dirty dishes and told to scrub them clean.

Refusing to be disheartened, she forced herself to think of her plan to go home. Surely she could wash dishes. How hard could it be? "Where should I fetch the water from?"

The servant who'd been tasked with getting Calista started, a plump woman Mr. Greene had referred to as Tilda, gave her an incredulous look and pointed toward the stoves. "There are the kettles. Soap's in the pail behind you."

Calista wanted to ask about a sponge or a brush, but Tilda was already walking away. Setting the tub on a nearby work bench, she wrinkled her nose and wondered how best to proceed.

"Well don't just stand there, girl," the cook snapped. "Get on with it or get out. We've not the time to rest on our laurels 'round 'ere."

"What do you expect from a fancy foreigner,

Mrs. Elkins?" a middle-aged man dressed in a dark suit inquired as he collected the plates that had just been prepared by a maid Calista took to be Mrs. Elkins's assistant. "I wager she'll be sacked before the end of the week."

Considering it was already Thursday, the comment did not bode well. Determined to prove herself capable and earn these people's respect, Calista dumped a measure of soap into the tub, then crossed to the stove and grabbed the kettle. Only to withdraw her hand with an agonized squeal as soon as she touched the hot metal.

Laughter erupted behind her.

"You don't belong in a kitchen," Mrs. Elkins said while Calista's hand began to sting from the burn. "The sooner you realize that, the better."

Calista cursed herself for her foolishness. In her haste to disprove these people's assumption about her, she'd only lent credence to their opinions.

Furious with herself, she snatched a navy blue potholder from a hook on the wall and grabbed the kettle once more. As soon as the tub was filled with steaming hot water and frothy bubbles, she pondered her next move. A space would have to be prepared for the clean dishes to dry on. She'd figure that out while she waited for the water to reach a more comfortable temperature for her hands.

Eventually, with a dishrag laid out, she considered the fine white porcelain dishes stacked on the table, smeared in leftover gravy and bits of food. Right. Best get on with it then.

Pushing her sleeves up, she grabbed the sponge she'd located under the counter, and proceeded to wash each plate with care.

"I need more plates," someone shouted from the other end of the room.

"Check with the new girl," Mrs. Elkins replied.

Calista froze. She'd only just started washing up a short while ago. She began scrubbing faster just as another tub filled with dirty dishes landed beside her with a clatter.

"Cor," a young man mumbled. "Is that all you've done this past hour? Sammy, come lend a hand here, will you? We need those plates now and this scullery maid is taking forever."

"Let's have a look then," a young girl said as she shouldered Calista out of the way. She surveyed the scene and turned to Calista with sharp disbelief. "You've not even finished rinsing them yet."

"Wha…" Calista stared at the tub filled with water and soap. "I'm washing them."

The girl clucked her tongue. "You mean to tell me you were planning to dry those off and let all the upstairs gents and ladies dine off of them after only one dip? Are you cracked in the head?"

Calista stared back at her, horrified by the pricking sensation now burning behind her eyes. She'd always believed herself to be well educated and smart, and yet she could not do a simple task like washing dishes properly. "I'm sorry. I thought—"

"Well you thought wrong and now there'll be a delay. Heaven above, if Mr. Greene won't have all our hides for this. Move over."

Calista stepped back and watched Sammy rinse off the rest of the dirty plates with swift efficiency. She piled them on the side of the work table, then filled an empty tub with fresh hot water and soap.

"Is there anything I can do to help?" Calista asked while doing her best to ignore the angry stares the rest of the servants were sending her way.

"You can toss the dirty water outside," Sammy said without looking at her. "If you're capable, that is."

Forcing back the tears, Calista picked up the tub and made her way to the door leading out to a courtyard beyond. She would not cry in front of these people. She refused to. And yet, the painful knot in her throat suggested she might do precisely that at any moment, so she rushed through the doorway, sloshing water all over the front of her gown in her haste to disappear from the kitchen and from the censure she had to face there.

Hopefully with time, her situation here would improve, she told herself as she rinsed out the tub at the pump. It was important to be positive and to remember all she accomplished by being here. At least she had a roof over her head and the means by which to earn the money she so desperately needed.

But as the weeks wore on, she realized the hostility she faced would not diminish with time. And while she now knew her way around the kitchen and had learned how to accomplish her chores in a satisfactory manner, she invariably felt as though she risked getting sacked at any moment. It was as though an axe hung over her head, ready to drop on account of the slightest mistake.

It hadn't yet, though Mr. Greene had certainly threatened her with that eventuality more than once. The last time being when a plate she'd been meaning to wash had fallen to the floor and shattered. It hadn't been her fault. She was certain of this. Rather, the blame belonged to a waiter named Richard, who'd been harassing her since her arrival. He'd walked past her spot and pushed the plate straight off the work table.

"Mr. Greene won't be pleased with that," Richard said with a sneer. The young waiter had been particularly cold toward her after she'd threatened him with a knife during her first night in the pantry. His advances had not been welcome. So he did what he could to take revenge.

"I ought to turn you out over this," Mr. Greene said when he learned what had happened. "Instead, I'll deny you the next month's wages."

Tucked away in the pantry later that night and

with the door barricaded against unwanted visitors, Calista swore she would start seeking other employment. The only problem was her breaks were limited. But when she finally did manage to get to an agency, the response she received was no different from the one she'd been given before. References were required and since her only work experience was as a scullery maid, she had no hope of advancing to lady's maid or governess. In fact, advancing to the next position as tweeny would take at least another year of experience, she learned.

Disheartened and unhappy, Calista returned to the Imperial. This was only temporary, she reminded herself and as such, she would simply have to make the most of her dismal situation. She sighed as she crept into bed that night. At this point she would gladly give up the cabin she'd hoped to purchase for her return to New York and settle for the cheapest passage available. It would in all likelihood mean she'd be traveling with the cargo and all the other poor souls who couldn't afford any better. But Calista no longer cared. All she knew was that she had to get away from the Imperial as fast as she possibly could.

ACKNOWLEDGMENTS

I would like to thank the Killion Group for their incredible help with the editing and cover design for this book.

And to my friends and family, thank you for your constant support and for believing in me. I would be lost without you!

USA TODAY bestselling author, Sophie Barnes, has spent her youth traveling with her parents to wonderful places around the world. She's lived in six different countries, on three different continents, has studied design in Paris and New York, and speaks Danish, English, French, Spanish, and Romanian with varying degrees of fluency. But most impressive of all - she's been married to the same man three times, in three different countries and in three different dresses.

While living in Africa, Sophie turned to her life-long passion - writing.

When she's not busy dreaming up her next romance novel, Sophie enjoys spending time with her family.

She currently lives on the East Coast.

You can contact her through her website at
www.sophiebarnes.com

And please consider leaving a review for this book.

Every review is greatly appreciated!